WHEN DEBBIE DARED

by
Kathleen Robinson

cover and decorations by
Jim Tadych

WHITMAN PUBLISHING COMPANY, Racine, Wis.

Library of Congress Catalog Card Number 63-17831

CONTENTS

1

Heart's Desire

Debbie Robyne counted the money for the third time. She had to be absolutely sure. If, after all those skimpy lunches. . . . Her mind closed against the grim possibility.

Two half-dollars. Three quarters. Twenty-two dimes and four nickels. True then! Fifteen cents more than she needed. Chuckling secretly, she cascaded the change into her red leather coin purse with a rich, delicious jingle.

This should prove to her mother that she was growing more responsible, better able to take care of herself and her affairs. This was important to Debbie. It gave her quite a glow.

She was now prepared to return to Hoskins' Jewelry Store and deposit her cash with a flourish upon the shining mahogany counter. Without blushing, she could meet the too-kind eyes of that too-sympathetic clerk. What's more, though hard to believe, there would be enough for a sundae at the Rolling Pin. She hadn't indulged in a sundae since the beginning of her rigorous saving program.

Thinking of the jewelry store with its polished glass cases of watches, pins, rings and bracelets, its tables of gleaming silver and racks of fascinating, rib-tickling birthday cards gave Debbie duck bumps. Add to that the heavenly aroma of hot doughnuts, coffee and chocolate floating in, around, and about the Rolling Pin, and what was left of the sunny May afternoon loomed bright and tempting in her big brown eyes.

She jumped up from the low rocker beside her bedroom window.

A cardinal, spilling its song from the branch of a nearby tulip tree, spread startled wings and flew away.

Debbie smacked at her dark, shoulder-length hair with a brush. The next moment she started down the hall to tell her mother where she was going. And why. Her steps were as light as a dancer's. In her heart lingered the echo of the cardinal's liquid song.

It was absolutely necessary to have the bracelet. At least *a* bracelet. *Imperative* was Carlotta's word.

Carlotta Ermine, a New York girl whose father had been transferred to the Midwest on some big city planning project, had attended suburban Karidale High since September. She had organized a club of "the most attractive girls in the senior class." Debbie, a junior, had been hysterical with joy when asked to join.

Loving the older girl blindly, dazzled by her sophistication, it had never occurred to Debbie that she had been chosen because of her remarkable knowledge of French, Carlotta's most difficult subject. When she decreed that each member must wear a bracelet of a certain type—glittering, jeweled and expensive—Debbie had started saving lunch money. A week ago she had been informed that if she didn't come up with the proper emblem by a certain date she would be out. O U T—out. She had no intention of making any such exit.

Carlotta was the most exciting girl who had ever lived in Karidale. She had frequently been taken out of her school in the East to travel in this country and abroad. She was older than the other seniors, beautifully golden, smartly dressed and, in Debbie's bewitched eyes, the ultimate—the final syllable of the final word. Debbie had repeatedly assured herself that she would shrivel and perish if Carlotta put her out of the club. It was the most important thing in life to be one of the sophisticates, one of the "inner circle." No need to contemplate catastrophe now. She was fortified against it. When her mother knew, she would be pleased and surprised that Debbie had taken care of the situation by herself.

Her father was a salesman at the Karidale Hardware Store. He had been given an opportunity to buy into the company and the president had agreed to arrange for monthly payments out of salary. Debbie's mother had been delighted and said it proved that George Robyne was at last appreciated. The size of the payments meant strictest budgeting to the very last penny. If her parents could take it, Debbie decided not to complain. She was determined never to ask for an extra dime again after her mother had had to refuse the money for a new ribbon hair band and had looked at Debbie with tears in her eyes.

These circumstances could not be explained to Carlotta. She would just have to wonder why Debbie's father hadn't given her the money for a bracelet. Carlotta didn't suspect that he knew nothing of the desire for it.

Starting down the hall to her parents' room at the front of the cottage, Debbie hesitated when she heard her mother's voice behind the closed door. Debbie hadn't realized that it was time for her father to come home. He left the store at four o'clock on Wednesdays.

"It doesn't matter, dear," her mother said nervously. "I shouldn't have brought the subject up at all. If I hadn't seen it in the window. . . ."

"Deb'rah," her father said in his deep voice that made the name sound like a caress, "it just kills me. . . ."

Debbie heard nothing further. She pictured her mother sitting on the old needlepoint footstool by the window, her gray eyes bright and loving, following her father's every move. The sun, slanting from the west, would touch her dark hair with golden lights. Her face would be flushed as always when she was nervous or excited.

Her father, two inches over six feet, would stop and lean toward her, a worried frown between his brown eyes, prematurely white hair upstanding from worried fingers combed through it. He hated the budgeting more for her mother's sake than for his own. Debbie hated it. Period.

Reaching for the doorknob, she changed her mind. She would not interrupt them by barging in.

"I'm off for the marts of trade!" she called gaily. That was her Aunt Em's description of the business part of the suburb. Debbie was crazy about her beautiful aunt, her father's sister, and frequently imitated her expressions. "Want anything, either of you?"

She loved her parents and was proud of them. Her mother was lovely looking and her father was tall and had an air that made him seem better looking than he really was. He was popular in Karidale and greatly admired by the businessmen. Mother was president of the only organization she belonged to, the Women's Auxiliary. They had elected her because they loved her potato salad, she always said, laughing. She wasn't laughing now. Neither was Dad. They both sounded sort of keyed up.

"I'll be back in time to set the table," she called. "Why not have supper on the back porch? It's getting really hot. Well, so long. See you!"

Dad opened the door and said, his brown eyes twinkling, "I presume you'll pass the Belmont place."

Dr. Alexander Belmont was an orthopedic surgeon with offices in St. Louis. He was the father of Alec Belmont, a senior at Karidale High and Debbie's secret love. Secret? Then what had prompted Dad's question?

She colored painfully and looked at the floor. "Probably," she said very low. How in the world had he found out? Nobody knew. But nobody. Not even Carlotta to whom, recently, she confided almost everything. What could she have done to reveal her secret? She raised her eyes and met her father's probing look. "It's on the way," she added a bit lamely.

"Sure." He nodded. "That's right. Maybe Alec'll be cutting the grass. Oh, come here, darling." He laughed indulgently and held out one long arm.

She moved quickly and leaned against him. His arm went around her. She was conscious of his deep devotion and responded to it.

"You're sweet," he said, bending his head to study her. "You look as if you might have had a Spanish ancestor in the dim past, though far as I know, no such existed."

Laughing, her mother turned from contemplation of something out-of-doors and said, "George! Don't be ridiculous. Spanish ancestor, indeed! What nonsense. Better brush your hair, dear, if you're going out. . . . I believe there's a robin's nest in the Martins' syringa bush," she added, leaning toward the window again.

Debbie looked up, smiled into her father's eyes, pushed away from him, and ran back to her own room and brushed her hair—very carefully. She studied her yellow dress, decided it would do, and started from the house.

The telephone rang. Debbie answered it.

"Debbie? Oh, I'm glad you're home!" It was Cynthia. Cynthia Maddern. She and Debbie had been inseparable prior to Carlotta's advent. "Can't you come over? You're getting so high-hat I never see you any more. What you doing?"

"Oh, Cyn, I'm on my way to Hoskins' to get the bracelet. Remember, I told you that Carlotta—"

"Debbie Robyne! You . . . you *goon!*" So saying, Cynthia hung up.

Poor Cyn. She was just jealous because Carlotta hadn't asked her to join the club. Debbie had promoted her but the older girl said no. It would be wonderful to have Cynthia. Debbie missed her. She hung up and forgot about everything except her important errand.

The bracelet meant more than belonging to Carlotta's club. It meant that Alec would *know* she was a member. In which case he might pay some attention to her. Surely, she thought in all innocence, if Carlotta considered her worthy of belonging, she must be a little attractive. Alec couldn't be aware that she was now of the "inner circle." He was apparently unconscious of the fact that Debbie Robyne lived on the same globe occupied by himself. But he could not fail to see the sparkle and glitter on her wrist. When her mother and father knew about the bracelet, they would be overjoyed for her to have it.

Knowing better than to ask for the car—Dad wouldn't let her drive except in an emergency of gravest importance —Debbie danced down the walk to the street. Gasoline cost money.

A tall blonde in a smart, two-piece blue dress approached the house. Her curly hair shimmered in the sun. She placed her slim blue-shod feet daintily but with purpose, speed, and grace.

"Aunt Em!" Debbie cried. "How darling you look! Your dress is smart as—"

"Made it, myself," Emily Robyne said, smiling and kissing Debbie's cheek. She turned around to be inspected, swinging an enormous straw basket.

"You can do anything! Teach French, memorize yards of poetry, sew like nobody else and be as beautiful as—as— oh, as you are!" Debbie finished, embarrassed. "Stay for supper?"

Aunt Em lifted the corner of a fresh blue tea towel. "I made salad and cookies. And here's another book for you. Deborah said you loved Katherine Mansfield's biography and I thought you'd enjoy this collection of her stories, *The*

Garden Party. I had my class translate "Miss Brill" into French. It isn't very long, chick, and I wish you'd take a fling at doing it. It's important to go on with at least one foreign language and you've a real gift for French."

"I've already read more books and translated more stories than any of the seniors," Debbie said, laughing and accepting the book. "Thanks, Aunt Em. Will you take it inside for me? I'll be back in a little while. See you!" She returned the book and ran.

"Don't be too long," her aunt called. "I have news!"

Debbie waved without turning around. She thought spring the most becoming season to Karidale. Lawns were fresh and green. Jonquils in borders danced in the warm breeze. Lilacs stirred and birds flashed bright against the sky. The lacy leaves of willow trees blew like pale green water flowing. There was the far-away clickety clack of roller skates and the distant drone of a plane. Power mowers whirred in nearby yards. She breathed the odor of new-mown grass and thought it the sweetest perfume in the world.

Did the fact that she had reached the yard being mowed by Alec Belmont deepen the sweetness? Debbie giggled. There he was, near the columned front porch pushing a red power mower as though it were weightless. His long football legs cut across the lawn like scissors. Grass made clouds of green dust in the air. With his head thrown back and his mouth wide open, he was singing at the top of his voice.

Debbie's footsteps slowed. He sounded every bit as good as a Metropolitan Opera tenor she had heard on TV. Or baritone, rather, she corrected herself. Alec's height, his proud carriage set him apart. He seemed much older than the other seniors, older even than Carlotta. It was said that he always had a project and never gave up until it had been completed to his satisfaction.

Everything concerning him—his scrubbed blond looks, his habits, his medical goal—appealed to Debbie. She guessed she was in love with him. She started to hum, a hushed, tuneless little song that leaped from her heart to her throat and lingered there.

How could he go barreling back and forth across the broad lawn without noticing her? Her yellow dress was plainly visible in the sunlight and shadow through which she passed. If he looked her way, she would wave. Fresh? Maybe. Bold? Hardly. Friendly? Sure. Her heart stepped up its beat and a rush of joy poured through her. But only for a moment. He didn't see her. Or if he did, he pretended not to. Her face flamed and she was close to tears. Tears! How childish! She fought valiantly for control, tossing her head and tightening her lips. Her little song was stilled.

His head still thrown back, his voice still loud on the afternoon air, Alec continued to cut the grass, apparently unaware of her throbbing presence.

2

Two Surprises

Silent now as her own shadow, Debbie sped along the street.

How could a world so lovely, so fragrant, abruptly lose its beauty, its flavor of sweetness? Her hair, dark and soft on her shoulders, danced as though careless of her mood. Impatiently, she shook her head and hurried on her way.

Turning the corner, she passed the printing shop. The thump and rhythm of the presses matched that of her troubled heart. Usually, she liked the smell of lotions, sprays, and perfumes wafted from the beauty shop next door. Today, it sickened her. At the threshold of a radio repair shop, the owner stood with a small transistor in his hand, idly flipping it on and off, spilling bits of syncopated music. Debbie tensed and walked faster. A shiver ran down her spine as she imagined dancing with Alec. She loved to dance. And according to Carlotta, Alec was tops. "You feel," the older girl had confided, "like thistledown blowing when he holds you and guides you—oh, marvelously!" Swallowing a lump in her throat, Debbie started to run.

On Karidale Boulevard, the shops were larger, more impressive. Hoskins' was among them, third from the corner.

She passed the antique shop with its cobwebby windows to the floor, and her eyes were drawn to the vast collection of objects inside, visible as through a veil—fire screens, brass andirons, wood chests, umbrella stands, small chairs, great deep china bowls colorfully decorated and a pair of huge covered rose jars. She wondered why old Mr. Fieldson never washed the windows. Surely, he would sell more if people could see clearly what was available.

Attracted by a glint of gold, Debbie's attention centered on an oval mirror propped against an oblong box of some dark wood. The scalloped frame was gold. It was beautiful. For some obscure reason she felt impelled to have a closer look. Did that mirror mean something special? Was it one of her signs? Her symbols? Or was she deliberately postponing the purchase of the bracelet and savoring for as long as possible what her mother declared the most delicious of all sensations, anticipation?

Denying the impulse to go inside the shop and inspect the mirror, Debbie moved on.

Old Mr. Fieldson was standing in the door with a cup of coffee in his hand. Carlotta's mother was a good customer and she had told the girls that he always carried a cup of coffee around with him, sipping and bargaining. Mrs. Ermine's explanation was that he did it to occupy his nervous hands.

Debbie reached the jewelry store and studied the gleaming plate glass window. Nestled among the small jeweled clocks, necklaces of colored beads and pearls, the bracelet, her bracelet—sparkling and alluring—beckoned. "Let me glamorize your wrist," it seemed to invite her. "Let my jewels glitter and wink and win the attention of Alec Belmont. I can attract him for you." She could almost hear the words.

Shifting her one hundred and ten pounds from one foot to the other, she put her fingers on her lips to still their trembling. It was out of the question to control the thick, excited beating of her heart.

People might consider it absurd to fret and fume so over a mere bauble. They wouldn't suspect its importance in the life of Debbie Robyne. Perhaps it wasn't very adult, and she longed to be adult—to be done with the uncertainties of this in-between age. She wanted to be older, more independent, and wiser. This was a time of incredible confusion.

Just then the gray-haired clerk with the too-sympathetic eyes pushed aside a black velvet curtain and reached into the window for the most beautiful of the little clocks, the most elaborately jeweled. She glanced up, met Debbie's eyes and smiled, much as to say, *Help yourself, it costs nothing to look.* Earlier in the week, Debbie had priced the bracelet and promised to decide about buying it later. Well, the time had come. She would prove to that charming clerk that she meant business. Entering the store, she allowed the change in her red coin purse to jingle.

The clerk slanted her a smiling look—she was showing the clock to a tall, stoop-shouldered boy—and said, "Be with you in just a minute."

Debbie nodded and looked at the boy a second time. Ring Putnam. A rather odd, shy, studious boy in the senior class. Everybody at High seemed to know who he was but nobody had anything much to do with him. He was always alone. Debbie decided that when he had concluded his purchase, she would speak to him with special cordiality.

He glanced up, saw her, nodded, and said something she didn't hear to the clerk. She picked up the clock, brought it to Debbie and asked a question.

"How do you like this? It's their housekeeper's birthday and she wants a clock. The boy seems devoted to her and wants her to have a really lovely one. He's an odd one, else *he'd* ask you."

"Oh, the darling! The clock, I mean, not the boy," Debbie said, blushing. "He's shy. Any woman would love it!" She started to tell Ring, but knew it would embarrass him.

She wandered away to look at the cards on a rack, feeling sympathy for a boy so alone. Before belonging to the club, she had been lonely, too. Oh, not like Ring; she had had Cynthia. But Cynthia had been forever dashing home to her invalid mother, and Mrs. Robyne would allow Debbie to go to the Maddern's apartment only on rare occasions.

How fortunate she was to be one of the "inner circle"! There were only four girls besides Debbie and Carlotta, the president—Regina Coste, Merry Lansing, Anne DuBois, and Grace Webster. Debbie had begged her to include Cynthia Maddern but the older girl had declared that she was going to keep the membership as it was.

"Six is plenty," Carlotta had stated flatly. "Instead of the Three Musketeers, we'll be the Six Muscatels!"

"What's a muscatel?" Merry had asked. "Is that a girl musketeer?"

"It's a French wine, silly!" Grace had laughed.

"French nothing," Carlotta had contradicted. "It's made from perfectly good American grapes—"

"We're perfectly good American grapes, too," Debbie had laughed. "Even Anne with her French name."

"We'll settle for the Six Muscatels," Carlotta stated.

It had seemed a delightful idea.

Debbie turned when the saleswoman said, "Shall I get the bracelet out of the window for you? I do hope you've found that you can have it."

Trying to be very adult, Debbie said much as Carlotta might have done, "You may get it."

The clerk moved away but not before she had given Debbie a look of pure astonishment. In a moment she was back with the bracelet. Dangling over the edge of a shiny white cardboard box, it twinkled and sparkled in the brilliant shop.

Debbie lifted it gently from its bed of cotton, searching for the word Aunt Em would use to describe it. It came to her very quickly, and she said, not meaning to speak aloud, "Amulet! That's it. A charm." She fastened it around her left wrist thinking that if Alec Belmont didn't notice her now, he could go throw himself under a truck. Even the thought was a betrayal and she was at once ashamed.

"Is it cash or charge?" the clerk asked.

"It's four dollars?" Debbie's attention was riveted upon the various charms—a lantern, a pagoda, a cabin cruiser, an anchor, a coffee pot, and a clock—all set with flashing, different-colored jewels. It was fabulous. Absolutely and completely fabulous!

The clerk touched carefully coiffed gray hair lightly. "Plus tax," she said quietly.

"But you said the price included the luxury tax!" Debbie said, controlling the desire to hold her fluttering throat. If she owed forty cents more she couldn't buy it. There just wasn't that much available. Nervously, she emptied her coins on the counter.

The clatter was one rarely heard in Hoskins' select store; it attracted considerable attention.

The clerk scooped up the coins and counted them as carefully as Debbie had done. "Sales tax," she smiled. "Eight cents. You'll have some change coming." She picked up the empty box and held her hand out for the bracelet. "Want me to gift wrap it? No extra charge."

Weak with relief, Debbie shook her head, unfastened the clasp, and gave up her amulet temporarily. Anxious as she was to wear it, she decided to carry it home in a package. She would show it to the family after supper. They would be thrilled to pieces.

Now she remembered Aunt Em's parting remark about having news. Debbie would bet it was a new boy friend. Her aunt was what she thought of as a *femme fatale*. What heaven, to be a *femme fatale!* Well, being one of the Six Muscatels and wearing a fabulous paid-for-by-herself charm bracelet around her wrist was a long and delicious first step toward it.

The back porch was shaded and perfumed by honeysuckle vines. A yellow-flowered cloth covered the worn, scarred top of the drop-leaf table. The tea glasses were from the dime store but their amber color harmonized. Debbie examined the effect after she had put the proper utensils in their places and thought it looked lovely. Her mother truly had a gift for making a place charming.

While Debbie poured tea into ice-filled glasses, Aunt Em mixed her salad of green beans, cucumbers, orange slices and radishes in a deep glass bowl. It looked crisp, cool, and colorful.

"I sneaked a peek at *Gourmet* magazine at the library," she said, "and found this recipe. Olive oil dressing, too." Holding the long wooden fork and spoon, her hands were graceful as she tossed the ingredients.

"Mother sliced some ham," Debbie said. "It's in the refrigerator. I guess we're about ready. She's on the phone about the next Auxiliary meeting. Where's Dad?"

"He's down by the brook. Want to call him, chick? I'll tell Deborah."

The family assembled and sat down. As Dad said grace, Debbie thought he sounded truly thankful for their blessings.

"Did you favor the marts of trade for some purpose, chick? Or did you just stroll through to give the villagers a treat?" Aunt Em busied herself, serving the salad.

"Oh, I had a purpose, all right. I'll show you later." She could hardly wait to exhibit her prize possession.

"Just a tiny piece of ham, George." Aunt Em passed her plate.

He looked at her for a long, intent moment. "Emily Robyne, you have that light in your eyes. I know it of old. It means news, spelled in capitals. Those beautiful blue eyes don't go wide and dark for nothing. Give, girl, give!"

"I'll bet it's another boy friend!" Debbie said quickly. "You collect them like other women collect pitchers or elephants or—"

"Debbie, hush!" Her mother laughed.

Blushing, looking lovelier than ever, Aunt Em said, "You still have your eagle eye, haven't you, brother dear? As for you, chick, you're right. It is a boy friend. This time for keeps. His name is Barrett Fairfax—"

"Fairfax?" Mother asked. "Same as your school."

"He's from England—"

A heartfelt cry left Debbie's lips. "Oh, not England! Please, please don't go way over there to live!"

Aunt Em had always been her champion. She had lived here until Debbie was twelve years old and was responsible for her unusual knowledge of French, books, and poetry. She had shared Debbie's room and they had talked many a night until Dad had knocked on the door and said, "Lights out!" in a tone forbidding argument. When Aunt Em moved to her own apartment—the upstairs of a big old house on the other side of the suburb—Debbie had been acutely aware of her own loss. She still longed for her aunt's return. No chance of that now. She was in her early thirties and, Dad said, it was high time for her to marry and settle down if she ever intended to do so.

"I'm not sure where we'll live, chick, but not in England."

"Emily, Emily," Mother said, shaking a finger and smiling happily, "you sly girl! When are we going to meet him?"

"Em." Dad covered her hand with his own. "That's

splendid news, my dear. If," he added, running his fingers through his white hair, "Barrett Fairfax is adequate."

"He ain't purty," she said softly. "But he's the salt of the earth. You'll all be crazy about him. We hope to be married in the autumn." She leaned toward her brother. "If you don't agree that he's well worth waiting for—"

"Where'd you meet him, Emily?" Mother asked. "Have you known him long?"

"His young sister's a pupil at school. His great grandfather came from England originally and it was he who established Fairfax Hall. That's why, when Barrett's business brought him to America, he sent Margaret straight here to school. She has the looks her dear brother missed. He's taken care of her since their parents died in a flu epidemic in Liverpool. He came about a month ago with a double purpose—to inspect a plant in St. Louis and to see Meg graduate. I've known him three weeks and three days."

Dad made an unintelligible sound.

"Well, you're the gal who should recognize the prize," Debbie said. "And I'm terribly happy for you. Now, could I . . . I don't want to horn in. . . ."

"You have something to show us, Debbie? Something you got this afternoon?" Mother asked.

"Aunt Em knocked it spang out of my head. Shall I get it? My bracelet, I mean. Not my head."

"By all means," Mother said. "A bracelet?"

"We have to have them for Carlotta's club," she called, running into the house and back with the white box. Unwrapping it, she said, "I've saved lunch money for, oh, ever so long." She spoke with what she hoped was pardonable pride. "I couldn't have bought it if it hadn't been on sale at Hoskins'." She put the bracelet on and extended her arm. "Isn't it something? I've never wanted anything so much in my entire life. I'd have shriveled and perished if I hadn't been able to get it. I'd have been put out of the club."

"I'd give a great deal if your mother could have the thing *she* wants," Dad said quietly. "She scarcely ever expresses a desire for anything. For herself, I mean. It kills me. . . ."

Debbie, bemused, dreaming, completely absorbed in the charm which would work such wonders in her life, heard her father talking but paid no attention to what he said. Her mind and heart had wandered far away.

"George, please!" Mother laid her hand on his and gave him her quick, lovely smile.

Debbie noted the gesture and thought vaguely how nice it was that her parents were devoted.

"What is it, Deborah?" Aunt Em wanted to know. "The thing you long for?"

By this time, Debbie was picturing the light of interest flaring bright in Alec's blue eyes. Unconsciously, she smiled and turned her wrist this way and that. He would ask her to dance. . . .

Her father took her hand and squeezed it. She blinked and looked at his white head bent to study the bracelet.

"Carlotta described the kind we must have," she explained. "I was afraid I'd never save enough, but. . . ." She laughed and twisted her shoulders. "I finally made it, since Hoskins' has a window full of stuff on sale."

"It looks rather— I'm glad for you to have it, of course,

but I hate for you to cut down on your lunches. . . ."

"You think I'm so irresponsible, I thought this one way to show you. . . ."

"You mean saving the money and not asking us for it. I must say that was extremely considerate, dear. Wasn't it, George?"

Dad nodded silently and released Debbie's hand. She thought he looked sort of worried.

Nobody seemed hungry. The meal was over almost at once.

Mother rose and started to collect dishes. "You must bring Mr. Fairfax to us at once, Emily."

Debbie got up to help. Under a willow tree in the back yard a thrush struggled with a worm. She watched until the worm had been pulled from the ground. To her surprise, the thrush ate a bite then flew into the willow tree and sang its evening song, leaving most of the worm untasted. The song was plaintive, appealing. So, in an odd way, was the scent of syringa blowing in from the Martins' yard.

Sighing in utter content, Debbie reached for her dishes and heard the promising melody of the bracelet charms.

3

The Magic Begins

The next morning, fifteen minutes before the first bell, Debbie raised her left hand to push the swinging door into study hall. Under her right arm nestled four books.

Carlotta was waiting for her. They had agreed that this was the time and place to plan the first club party—after the president of the Six Muscatels had inspected and approved the bracelet.

Fascinated by its beauty and glitter on her wrist, Debbie stopped to admire it, smiling to herself and turning her head from right to left in order to see the jewels in different lights. Because she felt certain that it would prove the *Open Sesame* to the important doors in her life, she would from now on think of, speak of, and dream of it as *Sesame*.

Surprisingly, as though from outer space, a strong masculine hand covered hers. The next instant long, unhurried fingers flipped the bracelet's glinting charms one by one.

Once, when she was a tiny girl, she had wandered away from home and been unable to find her way back. She remembered how she felt when Dad's hand reached out of nowhere and held her own. There was nothing paternal in

25

this touch. She might have been a young tree shaken to its roots in a storm.

And then a voice said, "Ve-e-e-ry cool, the bracelet. It can't mean—it does mean Carlotta's club. But you're no senior! You look about twelve years old!"

Sesame! The first door open, or at least ajar. He had noticed her.

She had heard his voice before, across a room or in a corridor. This was different. This time he was addressing her. His hand touched her hand. His head was bent to hers. She had never listened to a voice as thrilling as Alec's. In his words, tossed to her so nonchalantly, she fancied the clarity and beauty of the little brook running over shining pebbles at the back of her yard. She had a wild desire for him to speak her name. Debbie Robyne. Almost, but not quite, she heard how it would sound in that spine-tingling voice.

Afraid to draw a breath and dispel the enchantment, Debbie stood there frozen, unable to turn around or speak, wishing that by some miracle this moment could be prolonged into hours, days, weeks. She had a hunch that it would be some time before she was this close to him again.

"Sorry I startled you," he said, half laughing.

His laughter was a bright feather down her spine.

"I have a note for Carlotta Ermine. I know she's in there." Alec dropped his hand and reached into his pocket.

She managed to turn her head. Looked up at him. Seeing his eyes, she thought of lightning. Blue and wild. She blinked and nodded and felt an absolute idiot.

"Maybe you'd deliver it for me." He fished an envelope

from somewhere and proffered it.

He looked cleaner, more scrubbed than any boy she had ever seen. His blond hair, still damp from a morning shower, was inclined to wave softly. The sleeves of his fresh gray shirt were rolled above his elbows. So definite were his features that his profile looked almost hard. There was a faint smell of pine soap about him.

He leaned toward her regarding her with amused intensity. His face was thin with high cheekbones and his eyes deep-set under straight, swift brows. He looked extremely serious until he smiled. Now, his face crinkled delightfully.

"So," he said, fanning the air with the envelope, "seems you'd rather not deliver this."

Debbie was robbed of her breath, her speech, and her poise. She hated herself but couldn't help it. She would do anything for Carlotta! Run errands for her. Carry her books when Carl McKnight wasn't available. Help her daily with French translations. But right this minute Debbie couldn't move.

"Okay, brown-eyes, skip it. I'll give it to her." Alec flung himself against the swinging door and disappeared beyond it.

She gave herself a little shake. Her head felt as cobwebby as old Mr. Fieldson's windows. Had Alec actually spoken to her? Touched her hand? She couldn't believe it. For so long she had dreamed of meeting him. This wasn't right. It should have been by candlelight with the perfume of thousands of flowers and the music of a string quartet. Or in the moonlight with the ripple of soft wind through her hair and the fire in his eyes meeting hers. There was no romance in a school corridor full of hurrying pupils.

In the same moment, Debbie acknowledged that no matter where they had met, under what circumstances, it would have been, for her, a shining moment holding just the two of them close together in its radiance.

Once again Alec had flung himself against the door—this time from the other side. Debbie, who hadn't moved a muscle, was knocked down. Her books scattered half-opened at his feet.

"Holy Toledo!" he cried, stooping and looking hard into her embarrassed eyes. "I knocked you down! You're hurt. You can't get up." He took her hands and very gently pulled her to her feet. "Why, you poor brown-eyes." He held her for a moment, his blue eyes playing like lightning over her face. "I believe you *are* hurt!" He looked very grim.

She felt like a fool, sprawling all over the place before those gaping students, but she wasn't hurt. She started to reassure him when she remembered some advice from Aunt Em: "If there's anything male nearby, try depending on him. You may be surprised."

Blushing guiltily, Debbie decided to practice what her clever aunt preached. She straightened her shoulders and groaned. Not very loud. Just loud enough for Alec to hear. "Never mind," she said with assumed bravery, "it's not too bad. If you'll pick up my books. . . ."

"Here," he said quickly, "lean against the wall while I get them, then I'll help you to your seat. Maybe you'd better have a doctor. I could call my father—"

"Your father?" To her own surprise, Debbie was enjoying herself. She felt like a sophisticated actress. She cast her eyes up innocently. "Your father?" she repeated.

"Oh! You don't know who I am. My father's an orthopedic surgeon, Alexander Belmont. He could tell. . . ." Alec
was collecting her books, handling them with the care which
books deserved.

"I don't really need a doctor, Alec." She loved saying his
name. It sort of tripped off her tongue, easy and smooth. As
often as she had whispered it to herself she had never before dared speak it aloud. "If you'll just help me . . .
o-o-h-h-h," she moaned softly.

"Something hurts you!"

"Nothing," she said truthfully. "Nothing, really."

Mr. Lupton, an English teacher in charge of study hall
for the first hour, strode down the corridor, tall, thin, loose-
jointed, smiling his customary, maddening, secret smile.
"Morning, Miss Robyne," he said. His words were accompanied by tiny drops of moisture. Carlotta said he belonged
to the fountain school of expression.

"Good morning, Mr. Lupton," Debbie said weakly.

"You aren't feeling well?" He paused.

"I banged into the door from the room side and knocked
her down," Alec said. "She says she's not hurt but she looks
—I think she ought to have a doctor, sir."

"Oh, no, really!" she cried. This had gone far enough.
Her face burned. "I'm all right, Alec. There's no need. . . ."

Mr. Lupton held the door.

Leaning heavily on Alec's arm, Debbie made her entrance.

Carlotta was there, sitting at her desk beside an open
window, chin in her hands, eyes on a book open before her.

She looked up. "For the love of cranberries!" Her head went higher. "What under the light of. . . ." She seemed unable to go on.

"Tell me where you sit," Alec said to Debbie.

Mr. Lupton walked ahead, paying no further attention.

"Right behind Carlotta. I'm Debbie Robyne. Not quite so fast, do you mind?"

"I'm sorry! Holy Toledo, I'll say I'm sorry."

Slowly, with every eye in the room upon them, they approached her desk. Alec seated her with care and set her books down. He pointed at the envelope on Carlotta's desk, saying, "Carl asked me to give it to you. He's gone to the dentist with a toothache. Now," he addressed Debbie, "if anything's wrong, I mean if you find later. . . ."

"I won't." She gave him her most brilliant smile, thinking him the most attractive boy she had ever seen. "I'm sure I'm quite all right. Thanks."

"For knocking you down!" His wide mouth twisted.

"For helping me—"

"Knocking her down!" Carlotta cried.

A gasp of amazement swept the room.

Mr. Lupton tapped his desk. "Miss Ermine, if you please!" His eyes moved over the others. "I'll have to ask you all to be quiet. This is, in case you've forgotten it, a study period."

"The bell hasn't even rung—" Carlotta began.

The bell rang.

When it stopped, Carlotta started to address a remark to Mr. Lupton. Wide-eyed and eager, she opened her mouth but before she could speak, Mr. Lupton, nodding at Alec, issued an order meant to forestall further conversation.

"Go along to your own room," he said.

"Yes, sir." Alec spoke then to Carlotta. "Watch her, and let me know if anything's wrong. I . . . I hope she's okay." He departed.

"Now, *give,*" Carlotta whispered urgently.

"I was standing in the corridor and he banged into the door and knocked me down. That's all."

"All! Well, fancy letting yourself be *knocked down!* If you think for a split second—"

"Miss Ermine, that will do!" Mr. Lupton interrupted.

"Don't be silly," Debbie whispered. "You can't possibly believe I let him knock me down in order—" Secret giggles stopped her words. *I might have, at that, if I'd been clever enough to think of it.*

"Oh, I don't know!" Carlotta shrugged. "He's the most—"

"Miss Ermine! Miss Robyne!" A fan of drops. "I'll have to ask you both to leave the room. I'm sure you want to discuss the accident, so suppose you go down to the principal's office for the purpose." Mr. Lupton jerked at his bright blue necktie and gave his attention to filling a gold-banded fountain pen.

Debbie said very quietly, "I don't feel much like walking down those stairs, Mr. Lupton," and gave him an appealing, one-sided smile, still playing the part of an injured innocent.

He cleared his throat rather violently. "Very well. Then be quiet, both of you. Absolutely quiet!"

Debbie tried to concentrate on her English lesson. Her

class had been assigned Matthew Arnold's poem, "Self Dependence," to memorize. She couldn't get beyond the first line and said over and over to herself, " 'Weary of myself and sick of asking. . . .' "

Carlotta shoved her French lesson into Debbie's lap with a whispered, "For the love of cranberries correct this. You disappeared right after school and I couldn't find you anywhere."

"Oh, I'm sorry! I had to get my bracelet."

A moment later came a note from Carlotta. "I'll have a look at it later. Get my French. I don't know half those words."

Without resentment at the peremptory tone of the note, Debbie got busy. Gladly, gladly, she would do anything for her beautiful Golden Girl.

The second the period bell rang, Carlotta spun around and said, "All right, now let's see the bracelet. I only got a squint."

"If you know Alec Belmont, why don't you introduce him to your friends?" Debbie asked, keeping her left hand in her lap.

"Know him!" Carlotta said, tossing her shining head. "Only here, at school. Nobody knows him socially. None of the girls. Oh, once Regina had a small party and he came. I heard later that his father insisted because Dr. Belmont and Mr. Coste are golf partners. Alec danced once with each of us. Regina's mother saw to that. And is he out of this world! He spent the rest of the time with Regina's sick cat. He never comes to the senior parties. Doesn't give a toot about girls. Especially young ones," she added with arch significance. "He craves football and stuff like that. He was nice to you—he's going to be a doctor, you know— because he's interested in anybody who's sick or hurt."

"You don't know him any better than that? The way you go on about him! Why, you talk about him all the time." Debbie hoped her relief wasn't audible. "I should think Carl would be jealous."

"H'm! I can dream, can't I? Hold out your hand."

As they went to their respective classes, Carlotta approved the bracelet. Before they separated, a date for the club party had been set. It would be a buffet supper and dance. Only later, Debbie realized that the party had been planned and thoroughly discussed with Regina, Merry, Anne and Grace. Today, Carlotta had done all the talking. Debbie listened.

Now she said, "I dare you to invite Alec."

"For the love of cranberries, he wouldn't come. If he only would!" Carlotta rolled her eyes. "Why don't you take a chance and ask him, yourself!"

"Just because he was nice to me when he thought I was hurt? Don't be silly!"

"Oh, well, there are loads of boys," the older girl said airily. "I'll ask one for you. You've only double-dated, haven't you? I mean with kids at the movies and stuff like that."

Debbie nodded, consoling herself with the fact that Aunt Em's advice about the helpless bit had paid off. Giving Carlotta a dazzling smile, she left her to go to math class. "I'll finish the rest of the corrections for you in class," she promised.

"Don't you dare forget it! I could flunk French, you know."

"Oh, Carlotta, you know I won't forget," Debbie said, casting a look of fond devotion toward the other girl.

4

An All-Wrong Evening

On the night of the club party the Ermine residence blazed with light.

"It's so huge, so bright," Debbie said nervously as her father turned the car into the sweeping, flower-bordered driveway. *Control, control. Don't panic like an infant.*

"Ridiculous," he said, "having the meal so late. Most of us have our summer suppers while it's still daylight. Who does Carlotta think she is, a debutante or something?"

"She's awfully sophisticated, Dad. She's traveled a lot and lived in New York and, well, she's different from the Karidale girls. Come in and meet her? She's the most beautiful thing I ever saw."

"How come your mother hasn't met her?"

"Carlotta wants us here every day after school except when she has another date. It's the biggest house and she has simply scads of records and their cook feeds us. . . ."

"Of course I won't come in. You said I'd disgrace you."

"Oh, Dad!" Smiling, she leaned against him. "You know what I meant. The others are with dates and— But then, I'd be all shook up, I guess. You've only let me double-date.

Whatever would I find to talk about?"

"You'll find out when the time comes. Your mother and Emily think I ought to let you come home with a boy."

"Well, but, none of them will ask me. If I'd come with one. . . . You'd better pick me up. It makes me feel silly and revoltingly *jeune fille* but I think I'd rather, h'm?" It was forever cropping up, the confusion of this in-between age—wanting to be adult and yet secretly fearing the responsibility.

He stopped the car before the broad front steps. "Ten thirty?"

"Can't you make it midnight for once? Remember, these girls are seniors. Wait till I get the salad. It's Aunt Em's recipe. Her bowl, too; she lent it to me. She's even more glamorous than ever, isn't she? I guess it's being so happy." Debbie reached for the bowl.

"I think radiant's the word for Em. You dancing tonight?"

"Oh, yes!" Debbie said on an ecstatic breath. "Midnight?"

"Hang onto your glass slipper," he laughed. "Want me to carry that in for you, dear? Looks heavy."

"I can manage, thanks." She could imagine the howl that would greet her, accompanied by her *father*. Abruptly, she cried, "Dad! The dressing! I forgot the salad dressing. I . . . I forgot it. Oh. . . ." She didn't add that thoughts of seeing Alec had robbed her of all others.

Her father chuckled. "You'll grow up some day." His voice was gentle. "Here it is, dear. Your mother wrapped it and gave it to me and suggested that I let you worry about it for a bit, but you looked so stricken. . . ." He gave her the jar in a paper bag, blew her a kiss, and drove away.

Debbie stamped her slippered foot, turned it on a bit of gravel, and almost lost her balance as well as the heavy bowl of salad. "They think I'm a perfect *baby!*" she muttered wildly, and made her uncertain way to the steps.

All day long she had been suspended between reality and dreams. Saturday meant no school and Carlotta had phoned this morning and been mysterious about Debbie's date.

"You don't know him. That is, you haven't actually been introduced but you know who he is and he knows who you are. Carl asked if he could bring him tonight. You'll shrivel and perish when you see who it is. Oh, I know that's your own special expression, 'shrivel and perish,' but I like it and I'm going to use it."

"Be my guest," Debbie had said, flattered and excited. Alec Belmont! Carlotta meant Alec. Of course. Debbie didn't ask. She wouldn't mention his name. But she had lived through the endless day in a state bordering on hysteria.

Cynthia Maddern had called and begged her to spend the night. When Debbie told her she was going to the club party at the Ermine's, Cynthia had hung up without a word. Poor Cyn. She really was a doll and Debbie missed her.

The salad bowl was heavy and Debbie set it down on the second step, the jar of dressing beside it. She ran up the three remaining steps and rang the bell. Chimes sounded. Their music hung briefly on the still night air. She remembered Aunt Em's stories of the carillons in Paris, and wondered if she would ever be lucky enough to cross the Atlantic.

She looked about her. The place was like something out of *House Beautiful.* Sprinklers played on either side of the long driveway, their spray accenting the fragrance of hundreds of roses in borders. In the light from the porch the grass glistened like the jewels in her *Sesame.* A white-painted ornamental iron table and chairs were grouped to the left of the steps. Three-tiered iron racks held potted pink geraniums. Debbie turned toward the door as footsteps approached down the long polished hall.

It was dust-colored Merry Lansing—big, rawboned Merry with her loud voice and expensive clothes. Tonight she wore a white pique dress, perfectly plain, but what lines! Held at the waist with a scarlet patent leather belt just the color of her lipstick. To look at her, Debbie thought, you'd know she practically lived on horseback. An expert horsewoman, she went to Kentucky every summer the day after school closed and spent her time on her uncle's plantation in the bluegrass region. Riding—that's all she cared about. She was the only girl in Karidale who had ridden to hounds. Mother had voiced the suspicion that it was her ticket to the priceless friendship of "that Carlotta Ermine." Debbie didn't think that fair.

"You didn't bring the salad!" Merry shouted, opening the screen door, holding it wide. "The rest of us brought our stuff and Carlotta's cook has fried bushels of chicken and now you—"

"I thought one of the boys could get it," Debbie said, unconsciously reacting to Merry's voice and speaking more softly than usual. "There's heaps of it and it's heavy as the mischief. I left the bowl on the steps."

"Wait till you see your date!" Merry had the grace to lower her booming voice. "He's got a thing for you, he told Carl. Everybody's on the screened porch off the study, drinking punch. Come on, we'll send one of 'em for the salad."

Debbie had never been here at night. She had the impression of a great deal of light, huge vases of fresh flowers and deep, soft carpets. Somewhere a radio spilled dance music. She imagined herself floating across a lavishly furnished stage toward a door which would open upon a scene of blinding beauty and excitement.

She followed Merry through the lengthy living room and the book-lined study to the porch. Halfway across the living room, she heard his voice. *Alec's voice!* Unmistakable. Tingling. True then! With the fingers of her right hand, she touched the bracelet. *Sesame!* This was the most important, the most exciting night of her life. Praise be, she had begged to stay until midnight. Smiling with rare expectancy, Debbie joined the crowd.

Merry cried, "One of you he-men in condition go bring her salad in. She had to park it on the steps. You know everybody. Where's Carlotta?"

"Answering the phone," Anne DuBois said. "Long distance from New York, no less," she added. "Hi, Debbie! You look sweet."

Anne was a witch with laughing green eyes and gorgeous auburn hair. She had a talent for designing clothes and planned to go into business with a well-known St. Louis modiste. Tonight's orange and white outfit was one of her own designs in polished cotton with tiny white beads outlining the Greek pattern on the blouse front. Very effective.

It was true, as Merry said, Debbie did know everybody. But the one in whom she was most interested sat on a low footstool playing with a beautiful boxer named Kathy. He glanced up, nodded at Debbie and said, "She's a real beauty," meaning the dog. He hopped up. "Get you some punch," he said, wiping his hands very thoroughly on a clean white handkerchief.

"Thanks, Alec." Her lips were dry. Her heart whipped up a storm that threatened her poise. She was surprised to see Ring Putnam. She would have guessed him much too shy to attend a party. Meeting his eyes, she said "Hi" absently. Her mind and heart were with Alec.

Carlotta joined them, flushed and excited. Her golden eyes blazed and even her soft hair seemed to crackle. "Of all the. . . ." she stuttered, apparently unable to find the correct word to express her feeling. "A man I know in New York *telephoned* me for a graduating present! Ever hear anything so—so— He's flying to Europe tomorrow, that's why he called so far ahead of time."

"What a wonderful idea," Debbie said, her expression warm with appreciation.

"What's wonderful about it?" Carlotta spun toward her. "I can't wear a phone call, can I?"

Debbie laughed, thinking the other girl terribly amusing. Glancing at Alec, she saw that he was not amused. Neither was Carl McKnight, Carlotta's adoring boy friend. He straightened abruptly and his punch sloshed over the edge of his cup. Only the girls seemed to relish the humor of Carlotta's remark. Perhaps the boys hadn't heard it.

Alec handed Debbie a cup of punch. A simple courtesy, no more. Yet the cup might have been brimming with some magic elixir to put the stars in her eyes and lightning in her heart. His fingers touched hers briefly and a song trembled on her lips.

Ring Putnam approached, saying, "I'll get the salad, Debbie. Show me where you left it?"

She had expected Alec to offer. It was up to him, wasn't it, he being her date? Instead, he wandered back to the dog, seemingly absorbed in playing with her.

"Of course, Ring." Debbie drank her punch hurriedly, almost choking on a shattering thought. Could *he* possibly be her date? She set her cup down and stole a swift glance at him. Together, they went to the front porch.

"Bet you're surprised to see me here," Ring said in his shy, hesitant way. "First party I've ever been to. Know why?"

"Well, I guess you're just not interested in parties," she said uneasily.

He was awfully tall and thin. His shoulders were broad and seemingly too heavy to hold up straight. At school, there was always chalk on his clothes and ink smudges on his fingers, but tonight he was scrubbed and polished and wearing a good-looking blue suit and gleaming black shoes. His crisp brown hair was neatly brushed and his necktie properly tied. He looked altogether different. Even his expression was more alert.

"I didn't mean that," he said, putting his hand under her

elbow. "I meant why I came to this one." He leaned toward her.

Unable to speak for the fear that filled her throat, Debbie shook her head.

"I want to know you. I told Carl so. That's why he got Carlotta to invite me. I'm your date and I'll drive you home. I have my car."

Debbie would have liked to rip *Sesame* from her wrist and pitch it into the limbo of forgotten things. She was sunk. Abysmally, suffocatingly sunk. Ring mustn't suspect. He had made an effort to meet her. She must appreciate that and act accordingly. Thank goodness she hadn't asked if Alec was her date. As Mother frequently reminded her, there could always be found something to be grateful for.

Ring held the screen door. Debbie stepped onto the porch.

"It's down there on the step. I just couldn't wangle it. I'll get that bag—there's a jar of dressing in it. It's my Aunt Em's Chinese bowl and her recipe. She teaches French at Fairfax Hall. She's a real gourmet cook and can do—oh, just about everything! Beautiful, too. Perfectly beautiful. A regular *femme fatale*." It seemed imperative to talk. To make sounds. It didn't matter what she said, just so she could talk away that hideous lump in her throat before it dissolved into babyish tears.

"Will you let me drive you home, Debbie?" Standing under the porch light, Ring looked at her seriously. He had asked the question as though it was important.

"I asked Dad to pick me up," she said carefully, not wanting to hurt Ring's feelings. "You see, he brought me and"

—she glanced away from those intensely clear brown eyes— "I didn't know who my date would be and if I *had* known it was you, I still wouldn't have known you had a car."

"May I call your father and ask him?" Ring hurried then to pick up the bowl of salad.

"Of course," she said, clutching the dressing nervously. She was thinking that he didn't seem so shy now. He really was nice.

"Ted Hopkins, Regina's steady, is out of town, that's how come she asked Alec," Ring said, and Debbie feared he had read her mind. "Everything smells super, doesn't it? Roses all over the place. I hope we'll eat before long. It's late and I'm starved."

"I'll get the door." Debbie held it open.

"How about the movies next Saturday night? Go with me?"

Debbie gasped. She wouldn't commit herself just yet. She couldn't bear to. "I'll have to see, Ring. I mean, what the family's plans are."

"Try to make it. I'll take this to the kitchen. Give me that bag." He departed.

"See you by the punch bowl." She managed a smile and returned to the laughing, chatting crowd.

Alec came toward her. She tried not to widen her smile but she couldn't control the jigging of her heart. He brought her a second cup of punch.

"Tell me you weren't hurt the other morning, Debbie." He looked concerned. "And that your shoulder's okay."

"I'm fine, thanks." She sipped the cool, minty drink and held his eyes with her own.

"Good! See you." He ladled a cup of punch and gave it to Carlotta.

Debbie's only consolation was that he didn't appear interested. He was doing the polite thing, no more.

Ring came in, saying, "I called your dad, and he said all right but to be back by midnight."

This happy boy was not the shy, reserved Ring Putnam of High. What was responsible for the change? His hesitation in speech was hardly noticeable. His shoulders were more erect. Remembering something her father had said about one of the men at the store, Debbie giggled.

"Tell me," Ring said, leaning toward her.

"You're so tall." Debbie smiled. "I was thinking of what Dad said about one of his friends—that he'd be a right good-sized man if they hadn't turned up so much of him for feet."

Ring's laugh startled the others. They all turned in open amazement. Ring Putnam laughing? Unheard of!

"Something Debbie said," he informed them, smiling, and not repeating the little story.

Mrs. Ermine, her blond charm emphasized by crisp blue organza, came to the door and said, "Everything's ready, Carlotta. Buffet style, you know." She glanced about her. "You all look very charming," she said, nodding. "Debbie, your salad is out of this world! Such an unusual combination. Delicious!"

"It's Aunt Em's recipe. She helped Mother make it. Did you taste it, Mrs. Ermine?"

"I must confess I sneaked a bite. Come along, children, the casserole will get cold."

They went into the dining room.

Inside the doorway, Debbie paused. "This is the loveliest room I ever saw," she said. The moss green walls and shimmering yellow curtains appealed to her. And the table, set with silver candelabra and bowls of flowers, was beautiful.

"We do thank you," Carlotta bowed low, smiling oddly. "It can't compare to our dining room in Darien. The plates are at the far end of the table. It's late for you suburbanites, so take heaps of food; you must be starved. Personally," she added with a twist of bare golden shoulders, "I think it's *gauche* to dine early."

She pronounced the word *gauche* as though it were spelled *goush*. Debbie controlled her inclination to smile.

"We frequently dine very late," Regina drawled, imitating Carlotta's affected manner.

Debbie turned and looked at Regina Coste, noting as she did so that Grace Webster's gray eyes were dark with disapproval. Grace was a darling, brown-haired and giggly. Regina Coste was tall, slim, extremely stylish. Her light brown hair was straight and she was clever enough to leave it that way. Curls, which were adorable on Grace, would have been absurd on Regina. Her sherry-colored eyes were set beautifully wide apart but their expression was cold and haughty. She moved in a studied, boneless fashion.

"And where is Alec?" she asked now, apparently annoyed with Carlotta.

"Washing the dog off his paws," Carl said, laughing at his own foolishness. "He's got a fixation about cleanliness. Guess it's because he's going to be a doctor."

Carl McKnight looked enough like Carlotta to be her

brother instead of her boyfriend. He had been crazy about her since her first day at school. They would graduate together. After the summer in an uncle's newspaper office, Carl planned to go East to college, and Carlotta was anticipating a year in a French school. The separation didn't appear to bother her, but Carl refused even to speak of it.

Merry Lansing was going straight to Kentucky where she hoped to remain. Regina was entered at boarding school and would visit for three months in Maine before going to Connecticut. Anne DuBois had wangled a place with a good dressmaker as prelude to a career in dress designing. As for Grace Webster—dear, plump Grace with the curly brown hair and the giggles—she declared that she was going to marry her West Point cadet the day he graduated in June and "follow him around the world to all the wars on Daddy's money."

Of the Six Muscatels, Debbie alone had no definite plan for the summer ahead. It was imperative that she get a job —her parents glanced significantly at each other whenever she mentioned it—but she wasn't going to worry about it tonight.

The boys formed a line with the girls' plates in their hands. The girls waited in a group.

" 'He also serves who only stands and waits,' " Debbie quoted Milton.

At that precise moment, Alec entered the dining room and gave her a swift, surprised glance which she did not notice.

"I always liked that dress, Debbie," Carlotta said, fingering the yellow-flowered voile. "Very becoming."

"What do you mean, you *always* liked it?" Grace giggled. "You never saw it before."

"That's her fantastic imagination," Regina drawled. "I told her that Debbie had it last summer."

"I can't dress the way you all do," Debbie said, laughing uncomfortably.

"What are you doing this summer?" Carlotta asked, keeping a hostess's eye on the boys.

"I have to get a job. It worries me plenty because Mother and Dad don't seem to think me responsible enough to hold one that amounts to anything. But if I want to go to nurses' training school—well, I'll have to pay at least part of my expenses. I wish I could find something to do out here. That bus ride into and out of St. Louis simply defeats me. Standing up all the way more than likely. Are you flying to Paris right after graduation, or waiting till fall?" Like Carl, Debbie hated even to mention Carlotta's departure.

"Oh, darn Carl! I told him not to give me any of that casserole. It's much too warm," she said, frowning.

"You'll be missing something, Carlotta," Grace said. "It's asparagus and spinach with sharp Cheddar cheese sauce. Afraid of gaining a pound or two, sweetie?" Her question was teasing, not in the least malicious.

"Take more than a pound or two to catch up to you." Carlotta smiled when she said it but the smile reached neither eyes nor voice.

Without quite knowing why, Debbie was troubled. She had felt so sure that Carlotta could do no wrong.

"Regina, come fill your own plate," Alec called. "I don't know what you want."

"Here's yours, Debbie," Ring said at her side. "I put some of everything on it. I'll go back and fill mine. Let's take them out to the porch."

"No, you don't!" Carl called, laughing. "That's reserved for Carlotta and me. Hands off!"

"Okay, okay; no production, please," Ring agreed.

Regina whispered to Debbie, "Alec and I'll sit with you all if it's okay. Let's get the table in the study, shall we?"

The meal seemed endless to Debbie. Alec spoiled it for her at the start. Regina brought up the subject of the New York theater and mentioned having seen a certain popular and outrageous play. Debbie asked a question about it.

Alec laughed and said, "Better stay on shore, brown-eyes. That water's too deep and too muddy for your young feet."

He might as well have said, "You're just a baby. Not old enough or wise enough for this crowd." Oh, it was not unkindly said. There was no ill will in his words. But they devastated her. Completely. No need for her to cherish the faintest hope of Alec's attention. She was not about to get it. Debbie was ready and anxious to go home right then.

What was to have been the most wonderful night of her life was a flop. A dismal failure. What's more, there was no dancing. Nobody suggested it and Debbie didn't dare. She knew with deep certainty that Alec wouldn't dance with her. He wouldn't be caught with such a baby!

If she were older, or a coquette, she would try to charm Ring. The truth was it didn't seem worthwhile.

They drove home almost in silence, but before telling her good night, he asked again about the movies next week. And again Debbie said she would have to let him know.

"Thanks for the from-ness, Ring," she said, and managed to smile.

"The . . . ? Oh, I get you! From the party. You have a way with words, all right. And I heard you quoting Milton."

She stood there wishing and wishing that he were Alec and wondering and wondering what to say.

"You're sweet, Debbie."

She gave him the key and he unlocked the front door. As she started into the house, he spoke. "You won't forget about the movies?" he whispered close to her ear. "Gosh, but you smell sweet! 'Night."

She stepped into the house and closed the door without a sound and brushed wildly at her stinging eyes.

5

Qualms and Quivers

Debbie turned off the lamp left burning for her in the living room.

She kicked off her slippers and, carrying them, crept along the starlit hall as quietly as possible so as not to disturb her mother and father.

There was no sound from their bedroom. She felt sure they were awake. This was the latest she had ever been out, and the first time alone with a boy. No doubt they had been worried. Now, they could relax.

Grateful for the absence of questions which would have been unbearable to answer tonight, she undressed and got to bed. Finally, she went to sleep.

She awakened abruptly, hearing the scream that hadn't left her throat. That dream again! That hideous, frightening dream of looking out of a twelfth story window in a city apartment into a deep well of night blackness—the small square court around which the apartment was built. Her parents were visiting friends and had put six-year-old Debbie to bed. Something had aroused her, later. She made her way to the window, looked out . . . and down. Even now, she remembered the experience with panic and still dreamed about it when sorely troubled.

Shivering, in spite of the warmth of the night, Debbie felt as she imagined a survivor of a nuclear explosion might feel—eager to be put out of such suffering.

There were at least two contributing factors to her abysmal misery. Alec's indifference was one. He didn't seem impressed even by her membership in the Six Muscatels, and his pointed reference to her youth had hurt. And tonight for the first time she had felt in Carlotta a disturbing shallowness, a twisted sense of values.

Debbie had fallen victim to the older girl's unusual beauty and sophistication and had been flattered by what she interpreted as Carlotta's affection. Now, she began to wonder if such beauty might have spoiled her and closed her heart to everybody but herself. It was a disloyal thought. Debbie tried her best to banish it.

Neither Alec nor Carl had been amused by Carlotta's reaction to that long-distance phone call. Debbie wished now that she had not laughed; she had got into the habit of thinking that whatever Carlotta did was right.

Debbie was grateful for Ring's attention. He was a senior and he didn't seem to consider her such a baby. She knew nothing of his background but supposed that Alec had had more advantages and for that reason seemed older. Alec certainly had no time for her. He had, politely of course, made that painfully clear. She wondered how many girls at school, or in Karidale, or in the whole wide world were crazy about boys who didn't know they existed. She sighed and sat up in bed. The soft May wind blew across her face.

She must forget Alec. She shivered. That was out of the question. She had watched him play football, listened to his debates in the auditorium, sat entranced while he took the lead in various plays, read his articles in the school paper . . . and longed desperately to know him. From her point of view, Alec Belmont had everything she admired. He was even going to be a doctor, while she planned to be a nurse. Debbie threw herself back into bed and dug her tear-wet face hard into the pillow.

The memory of that dream kept recurring and she fought to keep it out of her mind. It made her a little sick.

Being in love at her age didn't mean a thing, she told herself. Girls fell in and out of love dozens of times. She would, too. Though she tried to convince herself that this was true, she failed. Mother and Dad declared that they had fallen in love while still in kindergarten.

There must be more to life than love. At the moment, she doubted it, but suspected it to be a fact. It was time she stopped mooning about a boy who considered her beneath his notice, and gave some thought to the one who liked her and wanted to take her to the movies. He hadn't been chalky or inky-fingered tonight. He'd looked every bit as well-scrubbed and dressed as the other boys. And he was the tallest of the lot. So thinking, Debbie closed her eyes and as dawn was breaking, fell asleep.

The next morning, her father said, "I'm surprised and pleased that you made it to breakfast, dear. Had an idea you'd sleep till all hours. You look a little pale. Up too late? How was the party?"

They were breakfasting on the back porch. Her mother had made waffles and Debbie surprised herself by being hungry. Last night she couldn't eat her dinner.

"Who is the boy who brought you home, Debbie?" Her mother asked. "Your father said he sounded very nice on the phone. Polite and"—she smiled—"eager."

"Ring Putnam. He's a senior. He is very nice. Has a nice car, too. The party was . . . I don't know, Dad. It didn't come up to my great expectations, somehow. But that house! At night, it's fabulous. Such beautiful lamps and so many of them. Great vases of flowers all over the place. And the food!"

"Did you dance?" Her father watched her closely.

Debbie shook her head. "We had dinner awfully late and it lasted forever. Nobody mentioned dancing. We walked out in the yard—the garden, rather, until Carlotta tripped and ruined her slippers. Sprinklers had been going all over the place. When we went inside, some of them played bridge and the boys wanted to examine Mr. Ermine's collection of masks. Grace and I . . . well, we talked."

"It doesn't sound too hilarious," her mother observed. "Was your dress suitable, dear?"

Debbie laughed a bit shakily and repeated Carlotta's remark about always having liked it, and Grace's comeback.

Her mother and father exchanged glances which Debbie didn't understand. She felt raw and exposed, and hoped that they would not sense her deep hurt and unhappiness.

They all ate waffles in silence for a moment.

"Did Carlotta say anything more about your bracelet?" Dad asked.

"I just remember!" Debbie's head jerked up. "She didn't have hers on!"

"Did the other club members wear theirs?"

"Yes, Dad. The others did. Funny. She made such a point about our all having them. Well," Debbie shrugged, "there's no accounting for Carlotta."

"I'm glad you have yours, anyway," her mother said. "You longed for it so. . . ."

"How about you, Deb'rah?" Dad asked, putting his knife and fork down on his plate and wiping his mouth on a checked napkin.

"George, please! I do wish you'd stop bringing that up. Makes me wish I'd never mentioned it. Don't you want another waffle? Debbie? How about you?"

"No, thanks. What are you two talking about?" She had a dim recollection of having heard something like this before, but it hadn't fully registered.

Dad pushed away from the table, reached up and picked a spray of honeysuckle and tucked it in Debbie's hair. He dropped a kiss on the tip of her ear. "Your mother saw something in a window and fell madly in love with it," he said. "I'm sick about it because it's the only thing she's ever expressed a desire for . . . for herself, I mean. I can't afford to give it to her."

Debbie had longed in just that way for the bracelet after seeing it in Hoskins' window. But that was nothing, less than nothing, to the way she longed for Alec's attention. *Sesame* had failed her after all. Poor mother! It was awful for her to be hurt. And as Debbie knew full well, wanting something desperately and not getting it did hurt. Plenty.

She put her hand on her mother's.

"What is it you want so much?" she asked gently.

"Oh, George, I could slay you!" Mother flushed, looked adorable and shook her finger at Dad. "Won't you promise to let the subject drop? I'm sick and tired—"

"Make her tell you, Debbie. She's so vague about it, I can't get the picture."

"It's not a picture." Mother laughed and poured the last of the batter into the waffle iron. "I'll give this to the birds," she said, "if neither of you will eat it."

"It'll crisp their beaks if they get a bite as hot as ours," Dad said. He left the porch with a final admonition to Debbie to keep on until she found out.

"Where'd you see it, Mother?" Debbie was thinking how different her mood would be this morning if Alec and not Ring had brought her home last night. Cool morning air smelled of honeysuckle. Church bells were ringing all over Karidale. The strange, peaceful hush of Sunday hung over everything—everything but her bruised heart.

"Won't you forget it, Debbie? I'd give anything if I'd never mentioned it. Something attracted my attention in Fieldson's window and I told your father how beautiful it was and how I'd love to have it. I could have cut my tongue out the next second, the way he looked. He's the most wonderful husband and father that ever lived. He'd do without anything in order for you or me to have it. Buying into the company is imperative. We mustn't do anything to make him think we regret his agreement about the monthly payments. It does cramp us. It means sacrifices, but. . . ."

"Nobody's complaining!" Debbie said shortly, adding

quickly, "Oh, I'm sorry, Mother, I didn't mean to snap at you and sound so cross. Just tell me what it is. Not that I can do anything about it, but I do want to know. So does Dad. You started it, you may as well finish it."

"Now, listen to me, Debbie. You know Fieldson's reputation as well as I do. His antiques are outlandishly expensive. Oh, they're worth the price; he has the best. But I couldn't possibly buy anything in his shop. I saw it in the window. The frame—" Mother spread her hands over her empty plate. "I'm sure it's gold leaf. Scalloped. Expensive as all— Get the phone, will you, dear?"

It was Aunt Em, wanting a blow-by-blow account of the party.

"The salad made a terrific hit. Carlotta had two servings, but I think she was more impressed by the gorgeous Chinese bowl," Debbie said, remembering how those golden eyes had widened when they caught sight of it.

"Deborah and I bet that a boy would bring you home, chick. Did we win or lose?" Aunt Em's voice was light and gay.

"You're the end! The absolute end," Debbie cried. "A boy did bring me home and I'll bet Dad wouldn't have stood for it if you and Mother hadn't briefed him. He remembered to bring the bowl. The boy, I mean. It's safe in the living room. Very becoming, too. And a million thanks."

"As many welcomes, chick. Let me speak to Deborah? I want to invite you all to dinner to meet my beau—"

Debbie's squeal interrupted. "It's Aunt Em," she called, wondering why anybody that old could have all the boy friends she wanted and more, while her poor niece couldn't even get the single one she longed for. "Mother? Come quick!" Debbie stood by the phone while a prolonged discussion took place. It ended with Aunt Em's agreeing to bring Barrett Fairfax here to dinner some night, provided she be allowed to furnish the meal.

"That girl," Mother said, smiling as she hung up. "She's so thoughtful and generous. She'll bring her beau here. Some night real soon."

"He'd better be good enough," Debbie said flatly. "Do I have to go to church with you and Dad? I'm not much in the mood."

"Of course you don't *have* to go, Debbie. When have we ever insisted? Unless you want to go, unless you feel the need. . . ."

I do feel the need.

"You're right, Mother. I'll get dressed. May I wait till tomorrow to change my bed?"

"Why didn't you change it yesterday? That's the time—"

"Well, I forgot it," Debbie said more crossly than she realized. "Do I have to wash the dishes?"

"*While* you're washing the dishes," Mother said emphatically, "I'll make a dessert. I saw a recipe in the paper and we happen to have everything on hand—including a dozen stale graham crackers." She turned and started toward the kitchen. "I do wish you'd be more responsible about your duties, Debbie. I don't want to have to check up on you. . . ."

"You wouldn't have known about the bed if I hadn't told you! I wish you'd stop checking up on me. . . ."

"Well," Mother said very quietly, "just see that it isn't

necessary." Her eyes were bright and loving as she spoke.

Debbie felt a sudden rush of affection. Home was wonderful and she had wonderful parents. Even though she could do nothing about getting whatever it was that Mother wanted, she would go to the shop right after school on Monday and have a look. She had sort of a hunch that she might come up with an idea.

6

Debbie Dares

On Monday afternoon as Debbie hurried to the antique shop she was feeling unaccountably expectant and excited.

She made no effort to analyze her feelings. She was following a hunch. The girls laughed at her hunches, her signs and symbols, but she had found to her sorrow that she had best heed them.

Dad kidded her and said she acted as if she were the seventh daughter of a seventh daughter. Mother was tolerant but amused. Aunt Em said that if you were the sensitive sort, gifted with "seeing around corners," you were several jumps ahead of the rest and should take advantage of it. Aunt Em was one of the rare ones; she understood just about everything.

Approaching the marts of trade from school instead of from home, Debbie passed different shops.

The window in the Woman's Exchange fairly glittered with ruby glass plates, pitchers, and bottles flooded in sunlight. The Little Card Shop was full of Father's Day cards and various ideas for gifts for Dad. Debbie had her father's gift ready and so paid scant attention.

59

Her Mother's Day gift had been a three-layer coconut cake. Mother, who doted on it but said it was too troublesome to make, had been delighted.

Debbie smiled, thinking that Dad would be overjoyed that she had put together his fishing flies. The owner of Karidale Hardware had given him the materials, but Dad complained that he didn't have time to do anything with them. The flies were difficult to make, and she had worked diligently and long, after having studied the process and illustrations in a book from the library. Some day, when she was a nurse, she would be able to give her parents the presents they so richly deserved.

No doubt it would seem absurd to anybody who knew her circumstances for her to even investigate the thing Mother wanted. But Debbie was driven by an irresistible force like a strong wind. She gave up to it and allowed it to carry her to the antique shop. Just before she reached the steps, she halted abruptly and clapped her fingers over her mouth.

Carlotta! Carlotta would be looking for her to help with her French translation. She had been depending more and more on Debbie, though she made a pretense of trying very hard to do it alone. Well, for once she would have to depend upon herself. Debbie had "other myrtle boughs to pluck," quoting Aunt Em.

She paused at the foot of the two broad, shallow steps and saw old Mr. Fieldson standing in the doorway with a cup of coffee in his hand.

"Good day, miss," he said with a slightly foreign accent. He, too, belonged to the fountain school of expression.

"Hullo, Mr. Fieldson." Debbie's eyes moved from him to the shop window. "My mother saw something she's very much interested in. . . ." There it was again, that glint of gold!

"Come inside, eh?"

"It's silly; I haven't any money, but I— Well, I believe I will." Debbie fairly flew over the steps, feeling like a leaf in the wind unable to control her direction.

He was very large and very dark with a round, twinkling face and brilliant little black eyes. "Look around, miss. Your mother, she has been to the shop?" He swallowed the last of the coffee and put the cup beside the telephone on a marble-topped table. For such a big man he moved quickly and without sound.

"It's something she saw in your window. No, she hasn't been here for perfect ages. It's in a gold frame. She said it looked frightfully expensive but that she'd love to have it." Carlotta would disapprove of such an approach. Her mother, a good customer, bargained by the hour, if necessary, to get what she wanted at something like her price. Debbie didn't know how to operate that way.

Fieldson made a sweeping gesture with both plump hands. "Have a look, miss."

Fascinated, she obeyed. The place was larger than she had expected. It was L-shaped, with a second room evidently taken out of the rear left corner. Furniture stood in a jumble—tables, chairs, a mahogany secretary like Dad's that had belonged to his mother, a beautiful little love seat upholstered in strawberry brocade. Against the back wall was a glass-doored cabinet filled with tall silver goblets, cigarette boxes, salts and peppers, and all sorts of silver and gold boxes, some with flashing colored stones. On a shelf along the wall marched a variety of rose jars and a pair of magnificent green and white vases patterned like Aunt Em's Chinese salad bowl. At the angle of the L was a large round table cluttered with china, lamp bases, and a soup tureen of what Debbie thought was ironstone. Carlotta's mother had bought a similar one from Mr. Fieldson.

"It's . . . it's fabulous," Debbie said softly. "I never saw so much—so many lovely things." Privately, she thought they would show to better advantage if clean. Dust was thick over everything.

"Been too busy lately to do much cleaning or dusting," the old man said with an apologetic lift of one shoulder. "More important things on my mind. You see anything you're interested in, miss?"

She had explained that she had no money, and yet he was as polite as though she were an old and valued customer. In spite of his reputation as a skinflint, Debbie began to like him. "I can't afford to buy anything," she said, holding his eyes with her own wide and honest ones. "But I'm dying to see what it is that Mother's so wild about. It's unheard of for her to want anything for herself. I'd give anything to be able to get it for her. I saw something in the window—a mirror in a gold frame. May I see it? Just look at it," she added with an appealing smile, "not buy it, mind you."

"You want to see yourself . . . ?"

His question was cut short by a sound from the back room, separated from the shop by dark red velvet portieres.

"What was that?" Debbie asked, recalling the lines of a

poem: "Have you ever heard the sunshine? It's in the laugh of a boy."

The old man's eyes no longer twinkled. The merry planes of his face had vanished. Patting his rough black hair, he said, "You look around, miss. I—I'll be right back."

Debbie's inclination was to follow him—to find out what was going on back there. It was none of her business; she knew that. But she had a frantic desire to see who was responsible for that lovely ribbon of laughter, golden as birdsong.

Mr. Fieldson returned shortly, his bowed head wagging anxiously. His plump hands were clasped tightly before him.

"Is it . . . is it a child?" Debbie asked timidly. "I mean that sparkling laugh. It's like—"

"You want to see, miss?" Trouble crouched in his little black eyes.

"May I? Is it a child? A little boy?" She shouldn't go into that back room. Goodness knew what could be there. But she was drawn as though by a magnet.

"Come!" Mr. Fieldson's voice reminded her of the church organ. He pushed aside a portiere with tarnished gold fringe and motioned her into the other room.

There was the smell of apples and coffee in the combination bed-sitting room. Her immediate impression was of disorder and clutter. Even on this sunny day the room was shadowed. One wide back window was covered by a closed Venetian blind. The glass panel over the outside door was darkened by a heavy piece of material. Gradually, as Debbie's eyes adjusted, she made out a small form lying on a rattan couch under a pale coverlet.

"Will you raise the blind? I can't see very well," she addressed the old man as she approached the couch.

The blind was raised with a metallic clatter.

"It *is* a child," she said gazing down at a child with dark hair and black laughing eyes—the most adorable little boy Debbie had ever seen. She dropped to the side of the couch and took his hands, smiling in response to his gleeful, impish face. "Who are you?" she asked gently. "Did you just wake up from a nap?"

He pulled one hand free, reached up and patted her cheek, and rattled off words in a foreign language. His eyes danced.

"What's he talking about?" She turned to the old man.

He shrugged. "My daughter's boy," he said. "She's married to an Italian. Gentilini. They live in Tivoli. She was coming, too, but at the last minute. . . ." He shook his head. "She cabled she was sending Gino to me for the whole summer. I had nothing to say, or to do about it. Next I knew, the boy was here. She put him on a plane in charge of a stewardess with my address stitched into his clothing. At the airport, the girl put him in a taxi and told the driver seven-six-seven Karidale Boulevard. First night the boy fell down and broke his leg."

"Oh, no!" Debbie cried. "He ought to be in a hospital." The poor little lamb, she thought. Alone in a strange place with no way to make himself understood. And so incredibly good-natured.

"He's been in hospital." Mr. Fieldson jerked his head toward the shop. "I been there, too, half days. You saw the dust over all my treasures? His cast is off now but he mustn't put his weight on the right foot yet. Fell down the back steps, mebbe running away."

"How terrible," Debbie said, trying to follow the old man's jerky sentences. "How old is he? About three?"

Mr. Fieldson nodded. "Talks a lot, but I don't understand."

She smiled. "I guess he doesn't understand you, either. He's awfully pale, isn't he?" She thought what the little boy needed was fresh air and sunshine. What a dreadful thing to happen to him. So little. So strange. And so miraculously gleeful in spite of it all.

"Gino," he said, twinkling at her.

"Hi, Gino. Debbie." She indicated herself. "Say Debbie."

His black eyes crinkled in amusement, and his head rocked on the pillow. "Debbie!" The name left his lips like an arrow.

"You darling, you darling!" She hugged him and pushed the tumbled dark hair off his forehead, immensely drawn to him.

"It's kind of you to be interested, miss. But there was something you wanted to see in the shop window? Fieldson got to be better businessman now, with Gino here. Expensive."

"Yes. Yes, of course." Reluctantly, she got up from the couch. It gave a loud, protesting squeal like a cat's miaow. Gino laughed. Again she heard the sunshine. She stooped toward him, longing to do something for him—to protect him. Protect him from what? From disorder and shadows. From lying day after day with no fresh air or sunshine.

With a last, lingering look at the smiling child, Debbie followed the old man from the room. She would never forget Gino's small arms held up to her beseeching her not to go. She couldn't dismiss the memory from mind or heart. As she entered the shop, she quoted her mother saying, "The frame—I'm sure it's gold leaf. Scalloped. . . ." She felt the strangest urge to return to the little boy.

"Mirror in the window, eh?" He fetched the one with the scalloped gold frame and set it against a marble lamp base on the cluttered round table. From the drawer, he pulled a piece of scarlet silk with which he wiped the glass clean. He stepped back, waved his hand with the cloth in it and said, "Most beautiful women from old country in there. Royalty. See yourself, miss."

"Oh, but it is beautiful," she said, feeling with deep certainty that this must be her mother's heart's desire. "The very most beautiful thing I ever saw," she continued softly. "It seems—this is crazy. It seems almost to have a life of its own. It's the loveliest, loveliest thing!" Carlotta would scorn such enthusiasm. She would have pretended no interest until she learned the price. Then the bargaining would have begun. "My mother fell completely in love with it. Is it horribly expensive?" Even voicing the question gave Debbie a chill. She waited, without breathing, for his answer.

"Look at yourself, child, in the glass." His voice was very gentle, but she wished he wouldn't call her child. She preferred miss.

"Why, I seem sort of . . . of different," she said, laughing at her own reflection. "My eyes . . . they seem bigger, and my hair has a real shiny shine. How . . . ? What . . . ? I mean, is there some sort of magic about it?" Debbie blushed in embarrassment. If *she* appeared so much better looking, just think how lovely Mother's reflection would be. Oh, she simply had to have it! "Is it . . . ? It must be much too expensive."

Mr. Fieldson ran his lower lip over the upper one. He closed his eyes and appeared to be in deep thought. He finally said with a spray of fine drops, "Sell it to you for sixty-five dollars. And that is greatly reduced. For you, child."

Wanting to cry, she laughed abruptly and shook her head. Her throat closed. She had made a complete idiot of herself. Never in the world should she have exposed herself to such humiliation, sign or no sign. Symbol or no. If she were older she would have known better.

At that moment, the boy laughed again, that lovely liquid cadence, sweet as a cardinal's song.

"Look," Debbie said on sudden inspiration, holding the old man's little black eyes with her own blazing ones. "I have a super idea! Your Gino needs somebody to take him out in the sun. To wheel him till he's able to walk. To be patient and sympathetic. I'll do it!" *Dad will have a fit and lecture me about responsibility and all that jazz. He's never wanted me to baby-sit. But how am I going to learn to be responsible if I never try?* "I'll come and take care of him for three hours a day, every afternoon till school's out. I've got to get a regular job this summer. An all-day job, I mean." She counted on her fingers. "Instead of paying me, you could credit me toward the mirror. Would you? Could you do that, possibly?" She clasped her hands earnestly and leaned toward him.

He twisted his full red lips, cleared his throat, looked at her and then away.

"Oh, please, Mr. Fieldson! Please! You couldn't find anybody who'd take better care of him. I'm crazy about kids. I'm Debbie Robyne." Her breath came in quick, shallow gasps. She pictured her mother's delight at owning the treasure and hoped desperately that the old man would agree. She closed her mind to her parents' certain disapproval. That would have to be ironed out later . . . if at all.

"George Robyne's girl?"

She nodded eagerly. "We live on Hawthorne—"

"Fine man, George Robyne. He wouldn't have any objections?" Mr. Fieldson scowled anxiously.

"You mean *you* don't have any?" Her voice cracked. If she could get the deal all set up, she would stand a better chance of being allowed to go ahead with it. She'd show them she could be as responsible as all get out!

"Child, child, if you'd do that for me, for my little Gino, take it along. The mirror. Fieldson be glad to credit you. With eyes like yours— Lay your dark, bright little face behind that glass with some of the crowned heads of Europe. Surely a lovelier pair of eyes was never reflected there."

"You doll! You absolute angel!" Debbie danced a little jig of joy. "He looks like you, Gino does. When you smile and your face crinkles up that way. Oh, thanks a million! You won't be sorry, Mr. Fieldson. You'll never be sorry. I promise." She felt all undone inside with joy. Only later would she realize what was ahead of her—what she must give up in order to fulfill her agreement. She had never been in debt before. Not even a nickel's worth. Well, this was not the time to worry. Take one step at a time. This moment was all joy. Without shadow. Then a shattering thought occurred to her. Eighteen days. Three hours a day. "That's only fifty-four dollars," she cried. "Oh, but I'll keep on eating skimpy lunches. I'll make it. I'll get the sixty-five dollars, you'll see. I saved enough to buy this bracelet for myself and I can save even harder—"

"We make a deal, Debbie and Fieldson. You owe fifty dollars."

"I can't let you do that," she began, blushing and knowing that she would be only too happy to let him do just that.

"Any woman in Karidale would jump at the chance," he said, laughing and shaking all over. "They all love to bargain. Fifty dollars. No more."

"What's his last name?" Her voice rose in joyous excitement.

"Gentilini. Gino Gentilini."

"May I take it now? The mirror?" Debbie was almost sick with excitement and something else which she refused to admit was anxiety.

"You got your car?"

"I walked. But it's not too heavy, is it? Oh, I hope not. Can't be more than two feet long. Let me see." Debbie picked up the mirror and was surprised and worried by its weight. "I think I can carry it. I can't wait to get it home. Mother will absolutely explode with joy. No, don't wrap it up. Be easier to carry this way, I can get a better grip on it. Tell Gino I'll be here after school tomorrow, if you can make him understand." *And if I can make Mother and Dad understand.* "Good-bye, Mr. Fieldson. I never in my life can thank you enough. You don't know how thrilled I am!" Leaning heavily to the left, Debbie walked out of the shop.

She started up Karidale Boulevard with brave steps, but before long her pace slowed. An ache began in her back, high up between her shoulders. At the corner, she stopped and set her burden on the sidewalk, leaning it against a telephone post while she balanced it and caught her breath. Maybe she should have called Dad and asked him to bring the car. But no. This was her affair; hers alone. After a few minutes, during which she was stared at and smiled at by passersby afoot and driving, Debbie picked up the mirror and trudged ahead. The ache between her shoulders grew more acute, sharp as a blade. Again, close to tears, she rested.

Wouldn't it be murder, she thought, to drop the treasure and break it to bits? She shivered and could not contemplate such an overwhelming calamity.

Slowly, and still more slowly, she made her way home. Dusk was dropping down like a great smoky blanket. The sun had almost set. She had never been so exhausted in her life. She was soaked in perspiration; it ran off her forehead in big drops and stood in beads on her upper lip. Her yellow dress was dirty and mussed from the mirror rubbing against it. She could think of nothing but a warm, soapy bath and a cool, cool shower.

What a sight she must be, with her hair all draggy and

damp and her clothes mussed and soiled. For once, she was glad that Alec was practically unaware of her existence. She would shrivel and perish if he should see her now. When she passed his place, she must hurry as fast as she possibly could, though she felt that there was no hurry left in her.

At that moment a car backed out of a driveway. Debbie waited to let it pass. She looked up idly. Alec was behind the wheel! He *would* choose this very time to depart from his friend's home. Her face flamed painfully. Her throat closed. Having no faint idea of doing so and hating herself the second she had spoken, she said "Hi!" in an unusually clear and loud voice.

Instantly, she wished that by some magic she could disappear from those bright blue eyes forever.

7

The Long Way Home

Alec's blue eyes widened. His lips parted in a smile of pure amusement. It was not a smile that said he was pleased to see her or happy that she had spoken to him so eagerly. It registered simply and solely his amusement at her appearance.

Debbie realized this. Anxious as she was for her mother to possess the mirror, she would have welcomed a fissure opening in the earth—a fissure wide enough to allow her to sink into it with her treasure. She was paralyzed by embarrassment.

"Okay, brown-eyes," Alec said. "Get in. You look beat." He sat there holding the top of the wheel in both hands, leaning toward her and regarding her with amused intensity. "I'll drive you home," he added.

The shadow of a tree fell across his face, leaving one eye, in a sudden shaft of sunlight, brilliantly blue-lit and dancing with mischief.

Once again she was robbed of her breath, her speech, and her poise. Drive her home! A door might have swung wide into a beautiful and fragrant flower garden. Her fingers tightened on the mirror. Even in the heat, the glass felt shockingly cool. She couldn't utter a single word. If only she didn't look so completely undone, so mussed and dirty and dripping wet.

"If you're going to get in, I'll load that mirror," Alec said with a touch of impatience. "Otherwise, I'll be on my way." He fiddled with something on the dash, still regarding her with that maddening expression.

Cars passed. Playing children called to one another. A power mower racketed nearby. The air was saturated with the odor of freshly cut grass. Debbie saw nothing, heard nothing, smelled only the breath of pine lingering around the freshly scrubbed boy who had offered her a ride.

He didn't really want to drive her home. He was just being polite to a tired, bedraggled girl who should have known better than to speak to him so familiarly. He would think her forward. The mirror grew too heavy to hold. She set it down rather suddenly and leaned it against a tree.

Alec's fist touched the horn ever so lightly.

Debbie jumped. He laughed. Her fingers slipped and the mirror began to slide. She dropped to the ground so quickly that she almost fell. With an audible sigh of relief, she righted the precious burden. Then, smiling, she glanced up at Alec.

He got out of the car, lifted the mirror onto the back seat and motioned Debbie up front. He slid behind the wheel and closed the door. "Tell me where you live," he said.

Any other boy would have asked her address. Alec demanded it. Her heartbeat quickened. Her smile deepened.

She recalled that he had never asked her a question. Somehow, that increased his already giant stature in her eyes. She pushed the soaking hair off her forehead with her right arm and pressed against the back of the sun-warmed leather seat.

"Nineteen seventy-seven Hawthorne," she said. "It won't slide off, will it? I'd shrivel and perish if anything happened to it."

"The very idea of lugging a thing like that," he said, not looking at her. "Much too heavy." He seemed to be giving his entire attention to starting the car and backing it over the walk into the street. Then he drove carefully and competently.

They passed a yard bordered thickly in jonquils. Two dark-haired little girls, one in yellow and one in green, were picking them. Suddenly, the one in green jumped back from the border. Then she laughed oddly.

"What sharp laughter," Alec observed. "Bet the kid was stung or bitten and trying not to cry." He shook his head.

"Sharp as a needle," Debbie agreed. "Threaded with tears." She didn't see the quick look Alec gave her.

In the next yard, a man carrying a gold-headed cane went slowly down the walk obviously in search of the evening paper. He lifted the cane in salute.

Alec waved and shouted, "Evening, sir!" with enormous respect in the greeting. "That's Gustav Nicholson," he said. "Very well known writer."

Debbie saw and heard but dimly. Her attention was absorbed by the boy at her side. Her attention! The very beat of her heart.

"That mirror must be worth one heck of a lot," he said. "Looks like a genuine antique. My mother's nuts about antiques. She'd really go for that."

"I've practically gone into bondage for it," Debbie said. "I certainly hope it's worth one heck of a lot."

"Bondage," he repeated thoughtfully. "Sort of an odd word for a . . . for you. I like words. You do, too. I can tell. And poetry."

She nodded, wondering if he had recognized her quotation from Milton. Exhilarated, she noted that he was taking a roundabout way to Hawthorne. She hoped that meant something. Suddenly, she became aware that the shadowy evening was heavily perfumed with cut grass and flowers. That it was livened by the shouts of children enjoying their before-supper play. Debbie chewed her lips until they hurt. Sweaty hands made fists in her lap. She turned toward Alec and started to talk very fast.

"Words? Yes, I like words. My Aunt Emily Robyne used to live with us—"

"She teaches my cousin French at Fairfax Hall. I should think you'd go there."

"Me? Can't afford private school. Anyway, it's for boarders only." Otherwise, she might have added, Carlotta would be attending. She had wanted to.

"I interrupted you. Sorry." Alec flushed.

"Aunt Em shared my room and we'd talk way into the night. That is, she talked and I listened. She taught me French from the time I could say mama. That's why I don't have to take it at school. She got me into the habit of reading and loving poetry, even translating English stories into French. She's beautiful and gifted and I'm crazy about her."

"That's how come the word 'bondage,'" Alec said, nodding sagely. "Could be you even know what it means." He glanced at her with one eyebrow raised, teasing her.

"H'm! It means going to old Mr. Fieldson, the antique dealer, for three hours after school every day till school closes, and taking care of his little grandson."

"To pay for the mirror!" Alec said. Surprise touched his voice. "I'll say this for you, Debbie Robyne, you'll go far out to get what you want. I'm like that."

"Oh, it's not for me!" she cried, off guard. "I got it for Mother. She saw it in his window and fell in love with it. It won't be so terribly long until school's out— Please don't tell anybody, Alec." She shook inwardly whenever she considered her parents' possible reaction to her agreement with the old man. "I mean, well, not for a while."

"I've been to his place with my mother but I didn't know he had a grandson. I've never seen the kid. Of course I won't tell anybody." He held up his fingers. "Scout's honor."

She hoped he didn't think her childish asking him to keep her secret. She did it on a hunch. "Gino Gentilini," she said. "I don't know how long he's been here. Poor little thing fell down and broke his leg the very first night."

"Then he's visiting. He doesn't live with the old man." Suddenly Alec's foot came down on the brake, hard. A large red rubber ball rolled across the street directly in front of the car. A small boy ran after the ball blindly. "They scare me to death, the little kids," Alec said. And to the boy,

"Watch it, fella! You don't want a broken leg!"

The child looked up, beaming, lisped "Thanks," and scuttled back to his yard.

Debbie was thrilled by Alec's quick reaction.

"He's from Italy. Gino is." She voiced his name with unconscious gentleness. "Flew over in charge of a stewardess. He's three years old. Perfectly darling! I love kids. I know all the ones on our street. Gino's the dream ship of the entire fleet. But so pale and thin. He needs fresh air and lots of sun. I'm going to see that he gets it."

"You *look*—uh—young for a job like that, seems to me," Alec said slowly, each word issuing rounded and thoughtful.

"I'm almost seventeen, and it'll be fun taking care of him," Debbie said defensively. "There! Turn right at the next corner." Secretly gloating over the long drive, she made no reference to it. "The littlest house on the block. Lots of yard and not much else. It's that white cottage with the crooked brick walk. Dad and I laid those bricks last summer. You ought to see the back where the brook—" She stopped talking abruptly, afraid that he might think she was hinting for him to look at it.

"I hope the kid had a first-rate doctor and that the bones were properly set." Alec sounded angry.

"Oh, so do I! The cast's off, but he can't walk quite yet."

"I wish my dad had taken care of him. Maybe he could have a look. But no." Alec shook his head, bunching his lips. "Old guy might be offended. He's sort of proud, Mother says. Funny old geezer. Has a rep for terrific prices."

"I like him. Do you like children?" Debbie asked timidly.

"Last summer, Dad let me work in his office for the first

time. With Phil Andrews, a med student at City College. Phil wanted the experience and didn't care a hoot about the pay. I didn't work, really. I was just there. When little chaps were brought in for examinations, I'd get them ready. Try to keep them from being scared. Some of them were petrified. Others smiled and laughed, gay as you please. Sure, I like kids—when they behave. I'm working there again this summer. I'm going to be an orthopedic surgeon, too."

Afterward, Debbie admitted that it was in this precise moment that her tentative decision to be a trained nurse had crystallized.

"Gino's one of the gay ones," she said. "Gay as a lark. He has the loveliest laugh I ever heard. Like a bird singing."

Alec shot her an oblique look and stopped the car before the cottage.

Debbie tried to see it through his eyes. The little place compared to Alec's splendid residence about as she compared to Alec: simplicity against sophistication. If she only knew how to impress him, to make him see her not as a child, but as an adult capable of handling situations with poise and *savoir-faire* instead of tongue-tied embarrassment.

Pulling her attention back to the cottage, she admitted that Dad took good care of it. The white paint had been washed clean, the grass mowed and neatly trimmed. Later, there would be his roses, gorgeous yellow ones in full bloom on either side of the curving walk. About this time of evening they would fill the air with their own distilled essence. Unconsciously, she took a deep breath and smiled.

"It smells yellow," she said. "Not pink or red or white, but deep, rich yellow."

"H'm," Alec said quietly.

She heard, or thought she heard, approval in the word. Her heart soared and beat a song up into her throat.

"Look," he said, "my grandfather has a farm not too far out of town. He has horses, cows, thousands of chickens— Toledo! how I hate chickens! Some day after school, I'll take you and the kid out there. He could get the sunning of his life. You like horses, I hope."

"I don't know anything about them. I've never been close enough to a horse to touch it." She wanted to tell him how wonderful she thought him. How generous and kind. But that would sound too childish. Too *gushing*, as Carlotta said. Only a rare boy would make such an offer. Well, maybe others would offer, but how many would follow through? Chances were that Alec would forget all about poor little Gino. She'd just have to wait and see. All-in-all, this had been an exciting and rewarding day—up to now. Debbie shivered in anticipation of breaking her big news to her parents. Then, pushing fear aside, she gave Alec her most dazzling smile, unaware that it flecked her dark eyes with gold.

Abruptly, he said, "Your place looks swell. All those yellow rosebuds. They're my favorite flower." He too appeared to breathe their fragrance, half-closing his eyes, inhaling slowly.

"Roses?" Her question was not quite steady.

"Yellow ones. Hope you can find somebody to take care of them while you're taking care of the boy."

She laughed. "Dad wouldn't let the finest gardener in Karidale within breathing distance of his roses. He loves them like babies and cares for them the same way. You may have seen him in the hardware store," she said with unconscious pride. "Tall, with thick white hair. . . ."

Alec snapped his fingers. "So that's your dad! He's great. Swell salesman. Sold me fishing tackle last year. I got it for *my* dad."

Debbie spoke excitedly. "I've made all his flies for Father's Day!" Her face was alight with the enthusiasm in her heart. "Some job! Have you ever put one together?"

Alec shook his head. "My hands. . . ." He spread them wide. "Too big."

"Silly!" She laughed, thinking them beautifully formed and strong with fine, long fingers. "If they're not too big for surgery, they're not too big for flies. And you know something?" She tipped her face, bright and perspiring, to his. "I'll bet it's about as hard to put one of those tiny things together as it is to set a bone."

"Oh, you—you—*innocence!* Now I've heard everything." Laughing, Alec got out of the car, slid the mirror from the back seat and carried it to the porch. Debbie trotted miserably beside him, trying to keep step and smarting under his words. He stood the mirror against the clapboard wall and placed a straight chair to keep it from slipping. "Ve-e-ery cool," he said, regarding it with approval. "Bet your mother'll be delighted."

"I certainly hope so, Alec. Thanks a lot for the lift. . . ."

His laughter rang out loud and clear. He waved and ran back to his car.

Did that laughter mean that he had driven her home because he felt that he couldn't avoid it after her familiar greeting? Or did it possibly register—well, pleasure?

Carlotta had probably been right when she said the way to get his attention was to be sick or injured. His interest then was in Gino. Not in her. The song in Debbie's throat was washed anew in tears.

But wait! He hadn't known about Gino when he chose the roundabout way to 1977 Hawthorne. He knew about him now. And if he took them to his grandfather's farm. . . . "Oh, Alec, please!"

Meantime, she must present her gift.

She held her head high and forced her voice to ring with gaiety as she called, "Mother? Dad? Come to the porch and see. . . ." She swallowed painfully and for a moment could not go on. No anxiety of hers must spoil this occasion for Mother. "Something for you out here; hurry! Hurry," she added with almost tearful urgency.

8

Aunt Em to the Rescue

Trying to calm her gnawing unease, Debbie waited. Dimly aware of gathering shadows, the fragrance of blossoming shrubs and the drone of a plane far above, she acknowledged that Alec's opinion of her was of her own creating.

True, the unexpected sight of him backing from a friend's driveway had been a shock. True, the way she felt about him was responsible for her greeting. But why, why couldn't she have said, "Hullo, Alec," instead of that loud, bold "Hi!" In retrospect, she didn't know whether to be glad or sorry. Only time would prove her wisdom or her folly.

She heard approaching footsteps and chatter. Aunt Em's voice! Good. Debbie was always happy to have her here and she hadn't come very often lately.

Mother stepped onto the porch. Aunt Em and Dad followed.

"There!" Debbie pointed dramatically to the mirror propped against the house wall. "It's for you, Mother. I bought it for you." She wondered if her words could possibly sound as exciting to the others as they did to her.

Thinking of her own enhanced reflection, she smiled mysteriously.

Mother's hand flew to her throat as though to hold back a cry. Her expression changed swiftly from amazement to joy to bewilderment. Color flashed in her cheeks and her gray eyes were almost black. She pushed aside the chair which Alec had thoughtfully placed, stooped and looked at her reflection. Her gasp registered surprised delight.

Debbie shivered with joy.

Aunt Em's blue eyes darted from her brother to his wife. Then she glanced at Debbie and moved to stand beside her, always her champion.

Mother straightened up and said, "Dear child, what do you mean, you bought it for me?" She pushed the soft dark hair off her forehead. "You couldn't possibly—"

"Oh, but I did! I truly did. Don't you worry, Mother; it's yours all right. For keeps." Unconsciously, Debbie stood more erect. If a doubt about her ability—not to mention getting her parents' consent—to fulfill her agreement with Mr. Fieldson crossed her mind, she refused to acknowledge it.

Aunt Em's hand cupped her shoulder. In those thin, strong fingers Debbie felt affection, pride, and approval. Over her shoulder she tossed an appreciative smile.

"Well, well, I'll declare," Dad said. His voice sounded flat. Lifeless. Debbie thought she understood that while he was delighted for Mother to have what she wanted, he regretted his inability to give it to her himself. "How do you propose to pay for it, dear?"

"Mr. Fieldson has the most adorable little grandson,

Gino Gentilini." She was talking too fast. Too urgently. Now that the time had come to explain, she was terrified. "His daughter's son. Almost three years old. She lives in Italy. He flew over by himself and the very first night fell down and broke his leg. He's had it in a cast, but it's off now. The cast, I mean," she giggled nervously, "not the leg. He can't walk for a while but he needs to get out in the fresh air and sun. He's as white as chalk, poor little kid. I . . . I've agreed to take care of him after school. Mr. Fieldson said I could. I mean, well, it's my way of . . . of doing it," she finished breathlessly. Her spate of words seemed to hang on the air between her and her parents like a threat. Her uneasiness increased.

"But, Debbie child, that's entirely too much responsibility," Mother said, frowning deeply.

"I'll be seventeen almost right away, and lots of girls. . . ."

"I appreciate your wanting me to have it, oh, more than you know. It's not altogether a question of age, dear. Rather of . . . of dependability. It's the most beautiful thing I ever saw, but I just can't— Oh, my precious child! My dear, thoughtful girl." Mother's eyes filled with tears and she took Debbie in her arms, kissed her and held her tight, a most unusual demonstration. "You can't possibly imagine how deeply touched I am, but. . . ."

"Mother's right." Dad's voice was no longer flat. It was stern. Positive. "The very idea of that old skinflint persuading you to take care of his grandson! I never—"

"He didn't persuade me!" Debbie cried, close to panic. "I had to persuade him. It's my way to get it for Mother. The only way I have, Dad. Please! I want to so very much."

Her hands locked behind her to control their trembling. Her throat was dry. Suddenly, she felt that she had had about all she could take for the day. What must Alec think of her! His approval meant everything. She touched her lips with her tongue and waited fearfully for her father's reaction.

Aunt Em spoke in her soft, dreamy way. "I don't want to speak out of turn or be officious, but . . . could be that you're both low-rating your daughter." She smiled at Debbie and allowed one eyelid to just barely droop in their special private signal of conspiracy. "You see, I can view this situation objectively. Perhaps taking care of the little boy may be beneficial in several ways."

"Name one!" Dad barked.

They all jumped.

"With your permission, I'll name more than one."

"Be my guest." Dad waved his hand. He looked deeply worried.

"First, the mirror for Deborah. She wants it terribly, as you can see. She ought to have it. This strict budgeting isn't easy, and she's never whispered a complaint. Second, Debbie may find that she's not as crazy about nursing as she thinks she is. She's always wanted to be a nurse. Fine, lofty ambition. And I'm sure she'd be a splendid one. But after taking care of . . . what did you say his name is?"

"Gino. Gino Gentilini." Debbie thanked Aunt Em with her eyes and admitted secretly that, no matter how difficult caring for Gino proved to be, nothing could ever dissuade her now.

"After taking care of Gino, she may decide that anything

but nursing is the career for her." Aunt Em smoothed her blue linen skirt over slim hips and took a deep breath. "Smells heavenly, the spring. How I love it!"

"You can't switch our train of conversation quite so abruptly, Em," Dad said. "Going to the shop every afternoon— For how long?"

"Three hours," Debbie said. She felt a little sick.

"Three hours!" Dad fairly roared. "Ridiculous! Far too confining. You'd find it more than—"

"Confining?" Aunt Em asked quietly. "She said the boy needed fresh air and sun." She linked her arm with her brother's. "If she sees that the boy gets it, she'll be forced to partake of the same, won't she?" Her smile was merry, teasing.

"Did you carry that heavy mirror all the way home?" Mother asked. She had been stealing glances at her reflection, obviously pleased with what she saw. "Debbie, dear, I've never been so . . . so touched. To think you'd give up every afternoon. For how long?" she asked with startling abruptness.

"Only till the end of school. It won't be so bad, Mother. Honestly, it won't. You never saw such an adorable little boy. Black hair and the biggest, blackest eyes. Always laughing. He has the most. . . . Well, when he laughs, it's like sunshine. Like a cardinal singing. I never heard anything like it. I told Mr. Fieldson that when school's out I have to get an all-day job. He understands that this is just . . . just. . . ."

"In order to get the mirror for me." Mother's voice shook. She held her lip between her teeth and for a moment appeared buried in thought.

"How *did* you get it home, dear?" Dad wanted to know.

There it was. The question she had dreaded. Nothing to do but answer it and beg him with her eyes not to tease. He had evidently discovered her secret, but it mustn't be revealed to Mother and Aunt Em.

"Alec Belmont brought me home," Debbie said, her eyes pleading. "He put the mirror on the back seat and I was petrified it might fall off and break. But it didn't," she added needlessly, twisting her toes.

"I'm relieved to know you didn't have to carry it." That was all Dad said. It was more than enough.

She was furious to feel her face burn. She took a quick step toward the house.

"Look, George," Aunt Em said seriously, just above a whisper. "Look at Deborah."

Debbie paused in the doorway and looked intently at her mother, thinking how perfectly lovely she was. Her eyes were dazzling. There was a sort of breathlessness about her. It made her seem young. She gave off bright little beams of joy and looked as though she were about to start singing. It gave Debbie a feeling she had never quite known before —a feeling something like she had in church when the organist touched the first chords of a favorite hymn and she knew that when she opened her mouth to sing, the notes would pour forth rich and true.

When she grew weary or disgruntled caring for Gino, she must remind herself of this look of Mother's. It would lift her over many a trying moment.

"Don't go, Debbie," Dad said, holding out a detaining

hand and bending his white head toward her.

She turned to him inquiringly.

"I don't approve of this scheme of yours, Debbie. Not for a minute. You're entirely too young to take on such a responsibility. You should have known, not wanting you to baby-sit, that I'd never consent. I'm sorry, dear. But we'll have to return the mirror and cancel out your deal with the old man." Dad was terribly serious. Grim, even.

Debbie's heart dropped. "But, Dad," she said in her most appealing manner, "you and Mother are forever telling me how irresponsible I am. How *young.* Can I ever *learn* responsibility without taking some?" She would absolutely shrivel and perish if he denied her.

"It's entirely out of the question." His words were cold. Final.

If I behave like an adult, maybe he'll change his mind. He expects me to go to pieces—to weep and carry on. Her head went high. Her eyes, very bright but tearless, met her father's in a long, steady look.

"What," he said in a poor attempt at levity, "no tears?"

"I absolutely begged and implored Mr. Fieldson," Debbie said with but the suspicion of a quaver. "I'd do almost anything to get the mirror. I know it won't always be easy. But, Dad, like Aunt Em said, just take a look at Mother! It's been a long time since she's been so . . . so . . . I believe the word is *radiant.*"

He glanced from Debbie to her mother.

"Well," he said, rubbing the back of his neck and frowning thoughtfully, "let's say you may try it for a few days, a week. With the understanding that if it's too demanding and you get too tired, or the boy's more than you can handle—"

"Oh, you angel! You doll!" She threw her arms around him and kissed his cheek. "It'll work out okay, you'll see. Oh, thanks, Dad. A million, million thanks. It's all set, then? I may keep my agreement with Mr. Fieldson? He's so adorable! Gino, I mean," she added, giggling.

Mother said, "Debbie, thank you with all my heart." Her eyes were bright with unshed tears.

Debbie was deeply moved. She had known that Mother wanted something—wanted it rather desperately. But she hadn't dreamed that possessing it would fill her with . . . radiance was the word that came to Debbie. No other would adequately describe that *lighted* expression. Debbie gave her a quick tight hug and flew to her room, certain that wings had sprouted on her heels.

Determinedly, she pushed anxiety from her mind and heart. Nothing must spoil the happy mood pervading everything and everybody. For the first time in her life, Debbie had made a conscious, deliberate sacrifice of herself and her precious time. She had made it for Mother. And in spite of an undercurrent of apprehension concerning Alec, and also concerning her job as nurse to a bundle of laughing vivacity, this night must be gay. Tonight was Mother's.

Tomorrow was another day.

To her own surprise, as Debbie undressed and prepared for her bath, she heard herself humming a rather gay bit of tune.

9

Woman of the World

Debbie left for school earlier than usual on Tuesday morning.

Anxious to share with Carlotta the good news about the mirror and her job—and to avoid the possibility of a bawling out by Mr. Lupton if she told her in study hall—she decided to walk across Karidale and call for her. They could talk things out before school.

Carlotta's car was in the shop. Carl was out of town. The president of the Six Muscatels would be on foot this morning.

Debbie carefully chose a way that did not pass the Belmont place. Turning into a side street of small shops and apartments, she heard her name called in a familiar voice— feminine, lilting.

"Debbie! Wait up!"

She turned, waved and called, "Hi, Cyn!" and waited.

Cynthia Maddern had been her closest friend prior to the Ermines' coming to Karidale. They were still friends, but Cynthia resented the girl from New York and called Debbie's devotion to her *unconditional surrender.*

"What you doing over in this part of town?" Cynthia asked as she came running, green skirt flying, auburn hair jumping on her shoulders. Her gray eyes were alight with joy. She was the brightest, most vital thing on this drab, uninteresting street. She looked scrubbed and fresh, carefully dressed and combed, and she smelled faintly of soap. Debbie knew that she had bathed her invalid mother, fixed breakfast and straightened the apartment before she left— and probably fixed Mrs. Maddern's lunch. Cynthia was really quite a girl.

"Well, I got a job yesterday and it was so unexpected and exciting that I'm going by for Carlotta and tell her about it. How's your mother, Cyn?"

"A job! Oh, Debbie, how super! What sort of a job? I'll bet you're the first girl to land one for the summer. Mother's doing okay, thanks. Tell me all about it, every single thing!"

Mother's doing okay, thanks. It was her invariable reply. Cynthia did her duty and she did it with high and cheerful courage. And she wanted neither sympathy nor praise.

"I don't mean a summer job. It's only temporary, till school's out." Debbie told her about Gino and her agreement with his grandfather, and swore her to secrecy as she had sworn Alec.

"You're really hepped up about it, aren't you? A little foreign boy. How about that! Maybe he'll teach you Italian while he's learning English. Ought to be wonderful, Debbie. Just your cupcake. I've always thought you'd be good with kids. I hope Mr. Fieldson will pay you heaps. Oh, but you told me! The mirror for your mother." Cynthia's steps slowed. "Do you begin to know your luck, Debbie Robyne?" she asked softly, her eyes lowered.

Debbie nodded, unable to speak. Pity for Cynthia and her mother filled her throat.

"Do you *have* to go by for Carlotta? Couldn't we walk to school together, you and I? We used to, before. . . ."

"Sure we can!" Debbie surprised herself by saying. "I've missed you, Cyn." She put her hand on the other's arm.

"Whew! Let's see your bracelet!" Cynthia examined each charm. "Real jazzy. You buy it for the club?"

"I saved lunch money forever. Almost starved." Debbie laughed. "But if it hadn't been on sale I couldn't have afforded it. Had to get a certain kind, you know. Carlotta wanted us each to have one." Wanted! *Insisted*.

The girls stood close together in the rippling shade of an old willow tree. Cynthia's auburn curls were bent over Debbie's wrist. For the very first time she felt a little self-conscious about the bracelet. She asked herself why. Was it the presence of Cynthia, simply dressed and unadorned that made the jewels seem too glittery? Or was it the fear that Cynthia might *think* them too glittery?

Suddenly Cynthia raised her head. "I wish Carlotta Ermine and her sophistication and her fourteen-karat looks had stayed in New York where they belong!" she cried. "She's got you told. But good. Oh, I don't give a whistle about the rest. They're seniors and rich, anyhow. But for *you* to fall for that jazz! It's just plain silly. Go on, Debbie," Cynthia pulled away, "you'd rather walk with Miss *Gold Bullion,* anyhow!"

"No, I want to walk with you, Cyn. Honestly I do." It

was relaxing, easy to be with her again. Carlotta wouldn't approve. And why not? Debbie wondered. "Taking your lunch?" she asked, noting the tin box.

"Look." Cynthia sat down abruptly on an apartment house lawn and opened her green-painted lunch box. "I made a coconut cake yesterday. Want a piece? You used to be crazy about it, but maybe by this time you only indulge in *petit fours* or *gateau*." Cynthia giggled.

"You nut! I made a three-layer one for Mother's Day—"

"Your mother's crazy about it, too? I've got an extra piece, if you want it. I always take two. That is," Cynthia shrugged, "when I take any. Which, I hate to admit, isn't too often." She unwrapped a piece and held it up on aluminum foil for Debbie's inspection.

Looking at Cynthia, sitting on the grass with her green dress flared about her and her face lifted so that the sun struck across it, highlighting a flock of tiny freckles on her nose, Debbie felt sudden homesickness. Cynthia was exactly her age, a little shy of seventeen, and didn't mind acting it. Imagine Carlotta dropping down in some strange yard and eating a piece of cake. Not for all the world would she be caught doing anything so childish.

"Go on, take a taste," Cynthia urged. "It's good."

"Break me off a little piece." Debbie nodded. "Imagine! This early in the morning. I just had breakfast, didn't you?"

"Hours ago," Cynthia said casually, and divided the cake. "Sit down. They won't care." She nodded toward the apartment building. "We won't hurt the grass or leave any litter."

Debbie accepted her half of the cake and ate it, standing.

"Best thing I ever ate," she said, giggling and wiping her mouth on the back of her hand. This was fun. With Carlotta, she rarely giggled. "Cyn," she said, suddenly serious, "you're such a *child!*"

Cynthia's gray eyes grew wide and dark. Her sensitive mouth trembled. She turned away from Debbie for a moment, then quickly snapped her green lunch box closed and hopped to her feet.

"I'm sorry, Cyn, for snapping at you that way. It's just that—"

"You listen to me, Debbie Robyne, and you listen with both ears." Cynthia faced her furiously, her eyes snapping fire. "Since Miss Ermine-Vermin came to town you act like you've lost your last hook and eye, swishing around with a bunch of rich seniors, trying to act so grown-up and worldly wise. So important . . . belonging to that dratted club! It's just plain silly and I'm pretty disgusted. Go on!" She gave Debbie a quick little shove. "Go on and amble to school with your fourteen-karat chum! Translate her French! I'm not in the mood for any more of your jazz today!"

She, Debbie Robyne, one of the Six Muscatels, one of the inner circle, had been told off by an outsider. Cynthia had really given her the business. What was that about Carlotta's French? Carlotta had been marvelous to her, asking her to join her select club, so why shouldn't she help with the translating which was so difficult for the older girl. Yet Cynthia hadn't been envying her at all; she had been disgusted. It was a bitter truth which gave Debbie pause. But only for a moment. Thinking further, she came to the conclusion that Cynthia's defensiveness had its roots in envy.

Naturally, she would do everything she could to hide it. Nonetheless, jealousy had surely prompted her outburst against Carlotta and the club. The early warmth, the relaxed delight of being with Cynthia once more, was gone. Again, Debbie was wholly Carlotta's girl. She started on her way to call for her and break her exciting news, refusing to acknowledge even to herself that Cynthia's snub had taken much of the joy out of sharing it with Carlotta.

A car driving by slowed and stopped.

Debbie glanced toward it and waved.

Ring Putnam called, "Hi, Debbie! Hop in and I'll drive you to school. You and that atomic redhead!"

Debbie opened her mouth to explain that she was going to Carlotta's when an odd, hushed sound drew her attention to Cynthia. With an audible gasp of surprise, Debbie noted the change in her companion's expression.

All anger, all hurt had fled. Her lovely, long gray eyes were brilliant. Her head, brighter than the bracelet in the sun, was tipped at a listening angle as though waiting for Ring to drop more jeweled words from his smiling lips. There was nothing coy about her. She was completely honest, completely without pretense. In that way, Debbie thought, Cynthia and Ring were alike.

And with that realization a plan was born. A delightful, beautiful plan.

She grabbed Cynthia's hand and pulled her to her feet. At the same moment she called to Ring, "Be right with you! It's Ring Putnam," she whispered.

"Oh, I *know!*" Cynthia's voice was a song, her emphasis revealing.

They ran into the street.

"Cynthia Maddern, this is Ring. . . ."

Back of his car an automobile horn honked impatiently.

Debbie shoved Cynthia into the car next to Ring and scrambled in quickly. Smiling mysteriously, hoping that her plan would work, Debbie felt very adult. Very woman-of-the-worldish.

10

The Gold Tarnishes

That noon, Debbie carried her tray across the lunchroom to the Six Muscatels' table.

She was anxious to share her news and swear the girls to secrecy until Dad gave her the green light on her job.

"Where's Carlotta?" she asked, depositing her tray. "She wasn't in study hall this morning." She sat down next to Anne. "Who has grilled cheese? It smells marv!" Smiling happily, Debbie looked around the table.

"I have the cheese." Anne indicated her plate. "You looked right at it. It's the one completely edible concoction put out by our genius cook." She tasted her sandwich. "Marv! We're forever stealing your expressions, Debbie," she added, twinkling. "Sa-a-ay! You look as though you'd struck a vein of gold. Give!" Anne tossed her magnificent red head and squinted laughing green eyes.

There was certainly something about red-haired girls, Debbie thought. Ring had called Cynthia atomic. . . .

Merry said, "Anybody know what's with our president? By the way, it looks as if Grace is missing, too. I'll bet they're up to no good together and loving it!" She spread her paper napkin with hands so lean and strong that they evoked a picture of a restless horse controlled by their expert handling.

"Carlotta called me last night," Regina said in her beautifully modulated, affected voice. "She sounded in high Q. I tried to get her to spill the big news but she informed me, rather toploftically, too, as I recall, that I'd find out all in good time. Cranberries! This ham has turned to elastic!"

"Stretch it out and let it snap back." Anne laughed.

"If you'd ever tasted Kentucky ham, you'd never settle for anything as pallid and limp as that," Merry said.

"It's awfully dry, isn't it? Kentucky ham?" Regina asked as though abysmally bored by the subject.

"Dry and nutty." Merry closed her eyes and took a deep, swooning breath. "My uncle carves it so thin it just rolls after the knife and curls up sweet as a kitten. Between halves of a beaten biscuit—"

"Kitten sandwich," Anne said. "Sounds delish!"

"Have a heart," Debbie begged, "I want to tell—"

"My very earliest memory of Kentucky is of his cook— he's had her thirty years—slipping me a warm beaten biscuit with a curl of ham and a hunk of fresh-churned butter, and a small, fat, very *fawncy* glass of cold, rich milk at bedtime. Mother says it's a wonder I didn't lose all my teeth the way they fed me between meals when I was little. Every time she sees one of those kids on TV running and panting about no cavities, she asks me if I brushed my teeth after dinner. Or lunch. Or whatever. *Still!* Imagine! You'd think I was six years old."

Debbie toyed with her hash, eating little. She wished they

would stop talking long enough for her to explode her news.

"Everybody's awash on the subject of teeth and diet," Anne was saying. "Makes me sort of sick. Takes my appetite." She got up.

"Where you going?" Debbie wanted to know.

"To get another hot cheese sandwich!" Anne departed. The others laughed.

"She's about as wide as an exclamation point," Regina said, frowning. "How can she eat like that without gaining an ounce? It's revolting!"

"Dad would say she eats so much it makes her po' to carry it," Debbie said, laughing. "Listen! I want to tell you— no, I'll wait till Anne comes back."

"Is that gray dress one of her own designs?" Regina asked. "I dote on that style—and the bright green belt! It's certainly different. She's sort of a genius, I guess."

"Have you seen her beige linen lace?" Merry asked, rolling her eyes. "Such lines! Million-dollar simplicity. She's going to make a mint, that one!"

All this talk about clothes bothered Debbie. She felt young and *gauche* in her old blue skirt and blouse. Mother assured her that the collar was especially becoming, but that didn't help much. At that moment the excitement and joy over her job began to fade. The others would probably think very little of it. They had so much—not only of material things but of style and manner. Poise. Maturity. She sighed and decided she wasn't the least bit hungry.

Then she thought of the mirror which had lighted up Mother's face so beautifully. And Gino with his laughing black eyes, his arms lifted to her, the touch of his finger on her cheek. And all the keen delight in the prospect of taking care of him returned in a rush. Gino and the mirror made up for an awful lot.

"I have some news," she began.

Anne returned, eating her sandwich, rolling her eyes wildly, and looking most terribly pleased with herself.

"Sit down. Hurry!" Merry said. "Debbie's about to burst with some colossal news."

"I *thought* you looked suspiciously aglow!" Anne dropped into her chair and leaned toward Debbie with a teasing light in her eyes.

"Well, it's big news to me," Debbie said eagerly. "And I—"

Carlotta burst into the lunchroom and flew to their table, fairly stuttering in excitement. She sat down, picked up Regina's glass of water and drained most of it, slapped the glass down on the table, tossed her golden head, and cried, "Hold everything! Hold every little thing!" One slim hand went to her throat and she gulped audibly. "You'll swoon! You'll die! You'll shrivel and perish!"

"Oh, come off it, Carlotta," Anne said, wiping her mouth on a fistful of crumpled paper napkins. "I, for one, have no faint idea of pleading for a share of your world-shaking news. I've devoured two entire grilled cheese sandwiches, absorbed a huge bottle of Coke, and I'm in no mood. . . ." She pushed from the table. "I'm about to exit laughing. . . ."

"I've been to the airport," Carlotta drawled deliberately, crinkling her golden eyes in anticipation of the others' reaction.

"And your New York fella"—Merry made a face as she

said "fella"—"bounced off a jet and scooped you up in his long Harvard arms and whispered—"

"Oh, shush, Merry," Regina said. "Go on, Carlotta. Don't be so mysterious. Either tell all or let it drop. Stop treating us like eager kids hanging on every priceless word."

Debbie was shocked. She sensed impatience in Regina. Impatience with their adored Carlotta? Impossible. She must be mistaken. Regina was accustomed to being in Carlotta's confidence and no doubt resented her present secretiveness.

"Grace was at the airport, too." She laced her fingers and rocked her hands back and forth on the table.

"Grace!" Her name left Debbie's lips in a whisper.

Carlotta turned to her. "At least *you* care," she said. "You're interested in what went on, aren't you?"

"Oh, we're all interested," Merry said. "It's just that we resent being butterflies in a net. You've captured our attention so make the most of it."

Carlotta took a deep breath and tossed her dazzling smile in Merry's direction. "I went to the airport with Grace and Mr. Webster. She's on her way to West Point."

"Alone?" Regina's affected voice cracked.

"Her father's with her. She's frightfully spoiled, you know. He lets her get away with murder. They're going to West Point and stay for commencement and the day her cadet graduates—"

"They'll be married!" Debbie cried. "Oh, how exciting! In the chapel, I guess. Grace says it's perfectly lovely. She's been there twice. Lots of cadets get married the day they graduate. Will she come back in time for commencement here? Will he come, too? Oh, I hope we can all meet him. He must be absolutely marv the way Grace carries on about him."

"Don't be silly, he's going overseas." Carlotta dropped her bomb with evident relish. "And she's going with him. Well, maybe not quite all the way, but as I said, her father spoils her to death and he told me if that's what his little girl needs to make her happy, that's what he wants her to do. Imagine! Just imagine!"

"You mean she's skipping our graduation?" Merry asked, big-eyed.

"And for a good reason," Debbie said softly, picturing curly-haired Grace as an adorable bride under crossed swords.

"Ha!" Carlotta exclaimed. "For a far better reason than you think!"

"What do you mean by that insinuating tone of voice?" Merry asked, giving Carlotta the benefit of a furious scowl.

"It's supposed to be a deep-dyed secret," she whispered, crossing her arms on the table and leaning on them, raising her brows and her shoulders in an exaggerated manner. Her eyes glittered.

"Then keep it that way," Anne said emphatically.

"If it's really a secret . . ." Debbie began.

"For the love of cranberries, she probably won't be back in Karidale for years. What's the difference? The secret is that she wasn't going to graduate, anyhow."

A shocked silence ensued for a full minute.

"She told you that?" Debbie asked. Her heart beat very hard. Her fingers twisted in her lap. It was supposed to be

older girl she had a strange thought. Fourteen karat, Cynthia had called her. But only twenty-two karat was pure gold, wasn't it? Debbie couldn't be sure. She wished the thought had never occurred to her. She obeyed Carlotta's command. There was no question of obedience. It would have been impossible for her to speak at the moment.

"For the love of your reputation," Anne said, her green eyes for once intensely serious, "sit down before you make a complete idiot of yourself." She tugged at Carlotta's green and white plaid skirt. Her hand was instantly slapped away.

"Think she's the one most likely to be chosen by an astronaut to fly to the moon with him?" Anne asked nobody in particular.

A subdued titter ran around the lunchroom.

Not one of the Muscatels so much as smiled.

Debbie wished the floor would open and suck her under it.

"I didn't know you were the sort to go blabbing everything you know to everybody within earshot!" Carlotta narrowed her eyes at Debbie. "But you are. You sure are. Though why the small assist with my French should appear such a big deal to you, I'll never understand. Never, never, never!" Her voice rose higher and higher. She pounded the table with her fist.

There was an uneasy shuffling sound throughout the room.

Debbie touched her lips with the tip of her tongue. Her throat was achingly dry. "Carlotta," she said very quietly, "don't talk that way to me." Her heart thumped painfully.

"I'll talk any way I please, Debbie Robyne!" The usual

cadence of Carlotta's voice was lost. "Just you remember that I am president of the Six Muscatels—"

"Oh, stop," Regina breathed. She covered her face with her hands.

"She's jealous," Anne said flatly.

Without taking her eyes off Debbie, Carlotta said scornfully, "Jealous! Me? Jealous of a girl who had to let a boy knock her down in order to meet him? Don't be absurd! And just because she happens to have an aunt who drilled her in French—"

"Jealous of Grace." Anne's eyes were almost black. "You're in a frenzy about it. You know," she continued more casually, "you're going to have to watch it, Madam President. Your gold tarnishes. But quick."

"You're responsible for all this!" Carlotta spat the words at Debbie. "You had to broadcast your knowledge of French to shame me. You've waited a long time to do this to me. You've been aching to cut me down, haven't you? Well, you just lend an ear. . . ."

Debbie was shaking all over. Had Carlotta injured her physically, the pain would have been less. This was a nightmare. She couldn't bear it. She couldn't. . . . Abruptly, she admonished herself not to be childish. Not to go to pieces. Not to let Carlotta know how cruelly she was hurt. Only by repeating these admonitions over and over to herself did Debbie achieve control. Unconsciously, her head lifted and she met those blazing golden eyes with her own, dark and almost steady.

11

The Wrong Knight

Ring Putnam, seated across the lunchroom, got up abruptly. He looked unusually brisk and alert as he stood tall and surprisingly straight for a moment. Then his long legs propelled him rapidly toward the Muscatels' table.

Debbie held her breath, wondering what he was about to do.

"Here comes your knight in shining serge," Anne whispered. She let one eyelid droop wickedly in the manner of Aunt Em.

Debbie's hands locked in her lap.

Carlotta, standing stiff and angry beside the table, her golden head held defiantly, made a short, unintelligible sound.

Merry gave absorbed attention to her lunch, pushing food this way and that, rearranging it and pushing it again. She ate nothing.

Regina batted sherry-colored eyes as though disbelieving the scene developing around her.

The silence in the room continued.

Debbie wished that everybody wasn't so concerned with

what transpired at this particular table. She felt paralyzed with shyness, realizing that the Muscatels together could always be counted on to attract attention. Most particularly Carlotta. If Ring came and spoke to *her,* every eye in the room would leave the president and focus on Debbie. She twisted uneasily in her chair, picked up her glass and swallowed some water, and forced herself to watch his approach. She was aware only of his height and his long quick steps.

He came and stood behind her and held the back of her chair in both big hands and said, "May I drive you home after school, Debbie?" He didn't lower his voice, and she was embarrassed, but touched and pleased by his championing of her.

Without turning around she said, "Thanks a lot, Ring, but I'm not going home."

Aware of Carlotta's start, Debbie decided to arouse her curiosity, if possible. "I'd love it if you'd drive me to the marts of trade," she said quietly. Hurt and shaken as she was, she had determined to hide it and hoped the tremor in her voice was not as audible to the rest as she feared. "There's somebody I want to—there's something—what I mean is. . . ." After a moment, she continued. "If it wouldn't put you out or be too much trouble. . . ."

One big hand landed hard on her shoulder. "It's a date!" Ring said, loud and clear. "Meet you by the side door right after school!"

She saw that Alec, too, was on his feet. She allowed herself the delicious thought that perhaps if Ring hadn't jumped to her defense so suddenly, Alec might have offered. She pretended not to be aware of him, though her heart rocked in what she warned herself was immature excitement. That emotion must be hidden, too. Twisting in her chair, she looked up at Ring and said, in an excellent imitation of Carlotta's bored drawl, "You're awfully kind, Ring. Thanks again. See you!" Dismissing him.

In the intense clarity of his brown eyes she read his understanding of the situation. Giving her a slightly conspiratorial smile, he returned to his table.

Conversation became general again and Debbie, relieved of the spotlight, could relax a bit.

"You know," Anne said brightly, "Ring Putnam's getting to be pretty nice. Who can tell? He may turn out to be a world beater. The quiet reserved ones sometimes do. He looks clean. Brushed. No more chalk. And his hands—by the way, they're huge but very well put together with fine, long fingers—were scrubbed. But good! He looked as if he'd like to hold your shoulders instead of the chair back. He's got a real thing going for you, hasn't he?" Her eyes were teasing but kind.

"He drove Cynthia Maddern and me to school," Debbie said quickly, "and I sort of thought . . . well, he called her an atomic redhead. There's certainly something about any girl with hair the color of yours. . . ."

"Oh, stop your babbling, you two!" Carlotta dropped into her chair. The shadow of anger lingered on her face, eclipsing its beauty. "Get me a grilled cheese sandwich, Anne?"

"I couldn't look another in the teeth," Anne said coolly. With something very close to a wink at Debbie, she walked out of the lunchroom.

"After all," Merry said, pushing dust-colored hair off her forehead, "we're not your slaves, Carlotta, though we've all spoiled you—bewitched by your beauty, huh? Which, perhaps I dare remind you, is only skin deep." Merry prepared to leave the table. A moment later she made a hasty exit.

"I'll get it for you, Car," Regina said, hopping up. "White, whole wheat, or rye?"

"White. Thanks."

From the first, Carlotta had made it plain that Regina was her favorite Muscatel, and she shared her secrets to a greater extent with her than with any of the rest. Their backgrounds of inherited wealth were similar. They had their own cars. They received fabulous allowances which put them in an exclusive financial bracket permitting smart clothes, theatre tickets, and all manner of luxuries.

Aunt Em had revealed the fact that they had tried in vain to register as day pupils at Fairfax Hall where only boarders were accepted.

Right now, Debbie wanted to get as far away from Carlotta as possible. But when she stood up she felt slightly sick and dizzy. She held the back of her chair for a steadying moment, then abruptly sat down in the seat, blinking and trying to focus her eyes.

Carlotta zipped open her cosmetic pouch of gold brocade. She applied fresh powder and lipstick, paying no more attention to Debbie than if she had been a spirit.

A spirit was what she felt like, drained of all vitality, all initiative. The buzz of conversation began again; the clatter of dishes, heard once more, sounded far away and gave her the weird sensation of going underwater. Carlotta's behavior had more than shocked and hurt her. It had revolted her. Her physical reaction was startling but understandable, feeling as she did about the other girl.

As soon as students, tables, the lunch counter and the big clock on the wall had stopped swaying and settled into their proper places, Debbie got up and ran as fast as her legs would carry her into the corridor.

She had passed a table of girls who had brought their lunches from home and were as usual trading sandwiches, cake and fruit, when she became conscious of eyes boring into her back. She whirled around to face Cynthia. A most unhappy-looking Cynthia whose lovely gray eyes were dark and troubled. Debbie realized that Ring's every word had been heard by every pupil in the lunchroom, including Cynthia. She was hurt. At the moment, Debbie's reaction was, *So that makes two of us.*

Later, she remembered what Dad had said about Mother's "working philosophy." "On the rare occasions when your mother is hurt or downhearted, she gets busy and does something for somebody in trouble. It always helps." *Okay, Debbie Robyne, do something for Cynthia.*

With this in mind she would greet Ring warmly, welcoming the opportunity to learn all she could about him.

Debbie found him waiting with a large chocolate bar and two ice cream cones.

"You don't eat enough," he said, passing her one of the cones.

"I'm not very hungry, thanks," she said, embarrassed but accepting it. Out of the corner of her eye she had seen Alec. He was standing half-turned away talking with two other seniors. He was very emphatic about whatever he was telling them, beating one fist into the other palm with a loud smacking noise. Though he did not turn around or change position, Debbie was sure that he had seen her—knew that Ring had been waiting for her. Of course Alec, too, had heard the invitation to drive her home.

"You in big trouble with Goldilocks?" Ring asked, taking a big bite of his cone and watching her closely.

Looking at him over the ice cream as she bit off a little, Debbie nodded. It made her sick to think about the trouble she was in with Carlotta.

"Don't let it bug you, Debbie. Go on; eat up, girl. You need nourishment." His eyes met hers and lingered. "Gotta eat this chocolate before it melts in this heat."

Did he know that she had been unable to eat lunch? Anne was right; he was getting to be pretty nice.

"Car's parked halfway down the block in a driveway—"

"Driveway?" she asked, surprised. The ice cream was refreshingly cool against her tongue.

"The people don't have a car and I rent their driveway. Keeps the car off the street. My uncle's sort of cranky about that."

They walked to the car, eating their cones and nibbling squares of chocolate. It was unusually warm and the air smelled of dust. All the lawns were covered with it and it seemed more like midsummer than late spring.

Debbie was trying to figure out the best approach to what she hoped to accomplish. Following the blow administered by Carlotta, she felt very kindly indeed toward Cynthia.

"There's the buggy," Ring said, indicating a yellow convertible parked in the shade of a giant oak tree.

"That's not the car you had the night of the party," Debbie said. "Cranberries! It's a real beauty, Ring. Looks missile-fast."

"Why, Debbie, it's the same car I drove you to school in this morning! Don't you remember?" Ring laughed. "It's one of the demonstrators. My uncle has an automobile agency. He's a bachelor and I live with him in a big old house a little way out of town. We have an old housekeeper who takes swell care of us. My parents are dead. I don't even remember them. I was only two and a half—"

"Oh, Ring, I'm sorry!" Debbie cried. "How dreadful for you. I just can't imagine not having Mother and Dad."

"You really love them, don't you?" He asked the question as though surprised.

That in turn surprised her. "Why, of course I love them! I'm crazy about them. Even if they weren't my own, I'd be crazy about them. I never thought of that before, but it's true. Poor Cynthia Maddern. Her mother's an invalid. It's terribly hard on Cyn, but she never complains or fusses, and she takes care of her mother and the apartment and—"

"No father?" Ring sounded but faintly interested.

"He's been dead for years. The poor kid doesn't even get to the movies very often." *Now that ought to give you an idea!*

"Hop in, Debbie. Want to drive? She's a real sweet job. Hold on, though. I told my uncle. . . ."

She smiled. "I'll bet you did. That you wouldn't let anybody else touch the wheel. I should hope not. Anyway, I'm too upset to even think of it. Thanks just the same." *Forget about being upset and concentrate on boosting Cynthia's stock.* "She works so hard, cooking delicious meals for her mother. She's a marvelous cook! Cyn, I mean. Not her mother."

"Ever see anything like that in Karidale?" Ring asked. "That man pushing a cart of flowers? Plants. Begonias, aren't they? Want one? I guess he's selling them." Ring backed the car out of the drive and headed for the business area. "Shall I tell him pink or white?" he asked as they caught up with the man.

"What? Oh. Oh, neither, thanks." She was always thanking him for something.

"Where do you want to go, Debbie?"

"Will you drop me at the Woman's Exchange?" Debbie didn't want any more people to know about her job. Not just yet. "I'm crazy about Cyn, but I haven't seen as much of her as I used to. I miss her. She and I used to—"

His sudden, rather explosive laughter startled her. *"La Ermine* could be to blame for that, I'll bet." He shook his dark head slowly. "She's not my dish. A bit too-too to suit plain old me."

Debbie was delighted to hear that. Cynthia was more his type. "You going to work this summer?" she asked.

"I'm going to sell cars for my uncle, I hope. I'm nuts about engines—anything mechanical. I'm going to take mechanical engineering at college. Time for a drive before I drop you?"

Your uncle has an automobile agency. You're going to work for him. What a perfectly scrumptious way for Cyn to latch onto some drives. She has a thing for you, Ring. I can tell. You two would have a ball together. I've got to get it going. . . .

"Did you hear me, Debbie? I asked if there's time—"

"Oh!" She came to with a jolt. "No, I'm afraid not, Ring. Where're you going to college? Or have you decided yet?"

He laughed as though amused. "Place I bet you never heard of. I'll tell you about it some time. Maybe Saturday night. You didn't forget about the movie, did you? I want to take you, Debbie."

She turned and looked at him, trying to picture him and Cynthia driving together. Her bright head would just about come to his shoulder. She was the same height as Debbie, five feet six. Ring must be over six feet. . . .

"You've blasted off for the moon or Venus without even a count-down, Debbie. You're in outer space again, not with me at all." He sounded cross.

"I'm sorry, Ring. I've had a real casserole of a day. My mind, or what's pinch-hitting for a mind, keeps wandering. What did you say?"

"Forget it!" He was angry. Or hurt.

"Look." Debbie leaned toward him. "I was rude and I'm terribly sorry. Please don't you start giving me the business. If you knew the things spinning around inside my head maybe you'd understand. I've been trying ever since noon not to cry and if you. . . ." She couldn't go on without dissolving in tears. And she would rather be hung by her little fingers, she told herself, than to cry.

"Sorry, Debbie. Sure enough sorry. You sure have had a

bad day and I won't dog you about the movies any more. But let me know, h'm? Soon as you can?"

She nodded. She was emotionally spent. Even the thought of Gino did little to cheer her. She was almost too beat to take care of him this afternoon. *None of that infantile thinking. You've got a job and it's up to you to hang onto it.* The memory of Mother's face when she saw the mirror for the first time helped to buck her up.

"Woman's Exchange coming up," Ring said. "Sure you want me to drop you here?" He pulled over to the curb and stopped. "Time on the parking meter, too. I can wait. What you after? One of those fancy flowered bowls in the window? I'll even break down and buy you one if that's what you want."

She wanted neither the bowl nor to find him waiting.

"You're a good cranberry, Ring, and I like you. But I won't let you buy me one of those bowls." Debbie shuddered and laughed. "Pretty terrible, aren't they?"

"Whew!" He exhaled noisily. "That's a relief! I was afraid you might have a yen for them."

"No, thanks. And I don't want you to wait, please."

"Don't forget to let me know!"

"I won't. And thanks a million." Debbie got out.

When Ring saluted, she waved. She was more fully convinced than ever that he was the boy for Cynthia. And if she, Debbie, was clever enough, she would give them each a push in the right direction.

12

A New Feeling

As Debbie walked the considerable distance from the Woman's Exchange to Fieldson's antique shop, she wondered how she was going to get through the rest of the afternoon. It seemed to her that the day had already lasted more than its allotted hours.

The combination of heat, hurt, and anxiety had contributed their part.

Glancing at a clock outside the bank, she noted that she was early, thanks to Ring. She need not hurry and arrive out of breath and in a drip.

The air was heavy, threatening rain. The sky had turned an almost brassy blue the way it did sometimes in summer. She hoped it wouldn't storm before she got home. However, the knowledge that she had lived through an emotional tornado was enough to brace her against the worst sort of spring downpour.

A radio somewhere in Engine House Seven was turned on full blast. The air was filled with the catchy melody and ridiculous words of the latest hit, "What You Gonna Say, Rebecca, When Yellow Leaves?"

"So long, I guess," Debbie said, unconsciously speaking aloud.

"So long," said one of three young Navy ensigns approaching with a swinging, carefree gait. "That's the password, isn't it?" He smiled engagingly at Debbie.

She blushed, smiled, and said nothing.

"Sweet brown eyes," the second ensign said, stopping square in front of her. "Attractive kid. . . ."

"But slightly whizzy." The third winked and nodded.

They pretended that they were not going to let her pass. If she moved to the left, so did they—to the right, they followed. Finally, one said, "Shall we dance?" and that broke it up.

Still smiling, she stepped to one side and continued on her way. She repeated, "Whizzy, whizzy, whizzy," over and over to herself. The Muscatels would be crazy about that word. But she must not think of the club or dwell upon the outrageous talking-to Carlotta had given her.

She dragged wearily on toward the shop. Her feet, in thin-soled pumps, were heavy as stones. Never before had she felt certain that her skin was tight-stretched over nothing. The thought was fascinating in a gruesome sort of way. As though she might suddenly take off for outer space and keep on going. What was it like way, way up there in the air, far above the earth? Debbie had never even been up in a plane, though she yearned to fly. Her thoughts were flying off at the strangest angles. She must pull them back to her destination and her job.

She found old Mr. Fieldson in a troubled mood. He paced around the shop muttering to himself in what sounded to

Debbie like incomprehensible legal terms. His face wasn't twinkling as she remembered it. He looked sad. His bright black eyes were deeply troubled. His step was slow and heavy as though he, too, were weighed down by unhappy thoughts.

She paused inside the door. "Mr. Fieldson? Anything the matter with Gino?" she asked timidly, almost afraid to interrupt his musing. She began to wonder how she had ever dared take on such a responsibility. Deliberately, she closed her mind to the possibility of failure. She had obligated herself and would see the obligation through.

The old man turned toward her. "Good afternoon, child." Even his voice was sort of dead. "Gino? No. No, the boy's doing very well. How about you? You look. . . ." He held his chin and studied her for a long moment. "You look kinda tired."

Cranberries! If he thought she was beat he wouldn't let her take care of Gino. "Tired? Me? Did you ever know anybody sixteen years old to get really tired, Mr. Fieldson?" *I never did—until now.*

Mr. Fieldson picked up a cup from the littered table, squinted into it, muttered, "Empty," and replaced it. His wise old eyes smiled. "No, child, I guess not." He waved her to the other room. "The boy's waiting, Debbie."

She parted the velvet portieres and poked her head into the bed-sitting room, wondering what could have thrown the old man into such a brood.

Gino sat on the side of the rattan couch, swinging thin little legs. He was eating a big round sugar cooky, spilling crumbs all over the floor. He looked up and gave her his heart-melting smile sweetened by grains of sugar.

The Venetian blind was all the way up. In the light from the small-paned window the room appeared in appalling disorder. Not dirty, just disarranged. An open ledger on an oval marble-topped table was about to fall. Debbie closed it and pushed it back to safety. She picked up some newspapers scattered on the floor and fluffed up the cushion in the only comfortable chair.

Her heart dropped at sight of Gino in mussed blue pajamas. She had expected him to be dressed and ready for an outing. Forcing a smile, she approached the couch saying, "How are you today, Gino?" She touched her chest and said, "Debbie," and wondered how she appeared in his three-year-old eyes. He looked like one of those ads for children's sleepwear, a tousle-headed imp with great black eyes. Or was it an ad for baby food?

There was silence while he devoured the last bite of cooky. He licked his lips thoroughly, held up his arms and, smiling, said, "Debbie!" and laughed that gay, rollicking sound that drove all thought of disorder and shadows from the room.

"You doll," she said softly. "You absolute darling!" She squatted on her heels and held his petal-smooth face between her hands. "Debbie's going to wash every single crumb and every grain of sugar off this pale, adorable little face and dress you up, laughing boy." For a long time she had begged Dad to let her baby-sit. When she was done with Gino, perhaps he would give in. *Done with Gino!* Debbie knew in her heart that she would never be done with this little wonderful boy. He would always remain in her heart a bright, laughing memory.

Mr. Fieldson entered the room slowly, bringing an atmosphere of deepest gloom.

Still on her heels, Debbie turned and said, "I'm surprised that Gino's not ready to go out. It's such a warm, sunny day. Hot, really. It's going to rain but not for a while. We could have quite a time outside and it would do him lots of good, don't you think so?" Poor old man; maybe he'd been too worried to think about dressing the boy. "He needs heaps of sunshine, Mr. Fieldson."

"Sunshine," he repeated in a hollow voice. He pulled an airmail letter from his coat pocket and tapped the envelope against his fingertips. "My daughter," he said, shaking his head. "Bad news." The tap, tap, tap of fingernail against paper was the only sound in the room. Dismal. Foreboding. "She sent the boy to me for the summer. Why? Because Gentilini lost his job and she has to go to work. Her husband, bah! Has tuberculosis. A cobbler! Cobbler! And my girl went to college."

"I'm awfully sorry, Mr. Fieldson," Debbie said. No wonder he was in a brood. "Would you like me to dress Gino and take him out?"

"I'd like for you to give him a bath first."

"A bath!" Her voice sounded odd in her own ears. "A— a bath?" she repeated more quietly. She had never bathed a child in her life. Or a dog. Or a cat.

"Don't look like that, Debbie. I know it's not part of your bargain. But today. . . ." His round old face quivered alarmingly and he looked about to cry.

Even though she was sorry for him, Debbie's temper

flared. Her job was to take care of Gino, not to bathe and dress him. She wished desperately that she had Carlotta's nerve and could tell the old man she wouldn't do it. However, she was afraid to tell him what she thought. She knew herself and just what she would do: follow his instructions obediently, though inwardly fuming.

"We-e-el-l," she said, getting to her feet. "I will, of course. Today," she added hastily. "Where's the bathroom? Where are his clothes?"

"Be sure not to let him stand, Debbie. That foot mustn't touch the floor quite yet. Bathroom's down the hall there," Fieldson pointed to a closed door. "You'll find clothes in the top drawer of a chest inside the room. Lots of clothes. All new. All colors."

"Washcloth and towels," she said, not looking at the old man. "Where are they?"

A moment later she carried Gino down the hall. In her fatigue she almost buckled under his weight. She seated him on a low stool while she ran warm water into a fantastic pink-painted tub on big curly feet. Vintage of the ark!

"Now, my wee laughing boy, off with the pj's and into the water. Debbie's bathed a doll almost as big as you are, but you're the first live creature. . . . Oh, Gino, sit still! I'm scared to death as it is and if you should take a spill on that leg. . . ." She lifted him and plumped him into the water.

He gurgled and laughed and smacked the water with his palms, shrieking gleefully when Debbie backed away from the resultant splash.

"You're the whizzy one," she scolded. "Can you say whizzy?"

He looked up at her, interested but uncomprehending.

"Whizzy." She puckered her lips and pronounced it very distinctly.

"Debbie!" he cried, splashing furiously.

"Say whizzy. . . ."

"Wizzy, wizzy, wizzy!" He started to throw himself around in the water.

Debbie grabbed him. She thought of the enormous doll Aunt Em had brought her from Paris for her sixth birthday. Debbie's chief pleasure had been to undress, bathe, and dress it up again. That was vastly easier than controlling this lively three-year-old. However, by some mysterious transfer of thought, she was able to make Gino understand that he must behave. He was perfectly angelic.

She soaped, rinsed, and dried him without mishap, then dressed him in cornflower blue shirt and brief pants. As she carried him back to the bed-sitting room she heard a familiar voice in the shop.

"Mr. Fieldson, if you do get that Chinese tea caddy and it proves to be what you hope for, I'd like to have the first look at it," Carlotta's mother was saying.

Debbie was very careful not to make a sound. She quieted Gino with a finger on her lips and seated him on the rattan couch. Not until the door closed behind Mrs. Ermine did she go into the shop.

The old man was standing with an empty coffee cup in his hand, staring after his customer and shaking his head slowly.

"Anything wrong?" Debbie asked. "You want me to take Gino out, don't you, Mr. Fieldson?"

"I was just thinking how some women spend their husbands' money, Debbie. Now, Mrs. Ermine . . . she's got more stuff than she knows what to do with." He shrugged fat shoulders. "Her whole house is full. . . ."

"I should think you'd be glad for her to spend it here!" Debbie cried defensively. "Besides, it's not necessarily her husband's money. I happen to know that she inherited a lot from her father. So I guess she has a right to do whatever she pleases with it." Debbie realized with a sense of shock that it was easy enough to stand up for somebody else. Why couldn't she do as much for herself?

"You're angry with old Fieldson. Can't say I blame you. I got no business discussing my customers, eh?" His beady black eyes almost closed. "I'll say this, child; you're exceedingly loyal. I hope your friends appreciate it. Gino all ready? Sure, take him out."

He showed her a small, two-wheeled cart at the foot of the back steps. She brought it in, settled the boy on the thinly padded seat and wheeled him into the shop.

"Looks pretty in blue," the old man said. He went into the back room. There was sadness in the very way the velvet portieres fell with a muffled shush behind him.

Debbie would be glad to get out and away.

At that moment, Alec and two of his pals walked past. Alec looked straight ahead. The other boys appeared to be talking to him at the same time.

Debbie saw them. That is, she saw Alec and knew the others were there. She felt safely hidden behind the cobwebby window. Next thing she knew, the old man would be telling her to wash that giant window. *He had just better not.* Following Alec with her eyes, she blushed painfully. Hating herself, she was aware of the hard, thick beat of her heart.

Alec would be noticeable in any group. Not for his size alone or for his appearance. There was a certain vibrancy about him, like a crackling electric current. He was terribly alive. He filled Debbie with a sense of expectancy, as though something exciting was on the verge of happening.

She leaned over to buckle a strap across Gino's lap.

He reached up and touched the corner of her eye with one finger, tipping his head and regarding her with black eyes as wise as his grandfather's.

"For the love of cranberries," she whispered, laughing shakily, "is it in my *eyes?* The way I feel about Alec?" She gave the little boy a squeeze. "Oh, Gino, Gino, I'm crazy about him! I guess I'm in love with him. He has everything! But everything. He's so straight and tall with such broad football shoulders. He's clean and scrubbed. Terrifically smart. In a word, Alec Belmont is completely marv!" If only he would pay some attention to her. If Alec instead of Ring had asked her to go to the movies Saturday night. . . . Debbie shook herself and whispered, half to herself, half to Gino, "I can dream, can't I?"

Gino's laughter washed over her, warm as sunlight.

She said, "Darling, Debbie's so beat, she's just going to push you around the back yard this afternoon. It's plenty sunny out there and that's what you need a lot of, my angel."

As she wheeled him through the back room, Mr. Fieldson, hunched over in the comfortable chair with the airmail letter open in his hand, said, "You're a good girl, Debbie.

It was a lucky day for Gino and me that brought you to the shop. Fact is, I don't know just how we'd get along without you. We need you, Debbie. Indeed we do. We need you very much."

It made her feel deliciously grown-up. Mature and responsible. To be needed. Nobody had ever said that to her before. But wait! Maybe the old man was just trying to placate her for having had to bathe the boy.

Well, she had no intention of being taken in by that!

The most she could possibly do to register resentment against the old man's imposition was to give him a look which she hoped would convey the bitter message she dared not voice.

13

"Grow Up, Debbie!"

Making her way home after her first day on the job, Debbie seriously wondered if she was going to be able to cope. Gino was a darling and she adored him. But even strapped into that cart he had been strenuous. It was impossible to imagine how much more demanding he would be on foot. But any doubt about her ability to control him must remain secret.

Maybe in a day or two, after the first severe effect of emotional shock had worn off, she wouldn't be so beat. In which case all would be well . . . she hoped. She must never forget Mother's delight at possessing the mirror. Debbie counted on that to lift her over many a hump.

She found Dad digging around his roses and whistling a tuneless air between his teeth. Mother said Dad was at his best out-of-doors "in the glare of the sun and the claw of the wind. Completely at ease under the open sky whether it poured sun, wind or rain upon him." Debbie thought his hands were splendid, made for digging and growing things in the earth.

The rosebuds were beginning to open a bit and to smell

that rich, deep yellow way. Debbie took a deep breath, remembering that they were Alec's favorites, too.

Dad looked up at her approach and said, "Why, hello, darling. How'd the job go the first day?" He pushed at his damp white hair with the back of a work-gloved hand.

"Golly, Dad, you look hot. You're dripping! How long you been out here in this awful air? We're in for a big storm or I miss my guess. I can't wait for you and Mother to see Gino. He is the absolute most. I'm just crazy about him."

Dad gave her a long, penetrating look, nodded and said, "Suppose you get a bath before supper, h'm? You look a bit warm, yourself. Call me when you're dressed and I'll get mine."

As she hurried into the house, Debbie was aware of his eyes following her. She loved her parents dearly and could not have expressed the slightest preference had she been asked. But Dad was the one with the X-ray eyes. He could look right straight into her and through her. He knew her every mood and temper. What would he do after recognizing her fatigue? Say nothing, and give her another day or two to get organized, or would he and Mother talk it over and decide between them that the job was too much for her?

She made her voice purposefully gay as she called, upon entering the house, "Mother? I'm home! Where are you?" Mother was an indoor person. Her eyes shone the happiest when she was in the house. Her hands moved without a lost motion when busy preparing food or sewing a seam.

"Sh! I'm on the phone."

"Oh, sorry!" Debbie tiptoed down the hall to her room.

She had an almost irresistible desire to fling herself across the bed and stay there. Without bath. Without supper. Instead, she undressed and went soundlessly into the bathroom.

"Emily Robyne, I don't want you to do that," Mother was saying into the telephone. "Of course my cooking is not in the same class with yours, but. . . ."

Debbie turned on the shower and heard no more. She was perishing to know what Mother and Aunt Em were discussing. She hoped it had something to do with Barrett Fairfax. Debbie was wild to meet him. What if he didn't prove adequate? Oh, but a *femme fatale* like her aunt wouldn't settle for anything but topflight.

Momentarily refreshed by the shower and clean clothes, Debbie joined her mother in the kitchen.

"Did you get along all right with the little boy, dear?" Mother was arranging slices of meat loaf on a platter with some of her wonderful potato salad. "Mrs. Martin brought us some fresh rhubarb and it made delicious sauce. Her brother has a truck farm."

"What were you telling Aunt Em you didn't want her to do? Yes, I got along fine with Gino. He's perfectly adorable." Debbie sat down and put her elbows on the kitchen table and watched her mother's marvelously sure hands.

"Oh!" Mother looked up, smiling happily. The smile went all the way up into her gray eyes. "She's bringing her fiancé to dinner a week from Friday. She insists upon cooking it. Most thoughtful girl in the world, that sister of your father's. She never for one minute forgets that we're budgeting, and she does everything possible to help. Perhaps,"

Mother added, hunching slim shoulders, "she doesn't like my cooking."

"Don't be silly! You're a magnif cook and you know it!" Debbie rested her chin in her palms. She ached from the back of her neck to the tip of her spine. Her legs felt as though they had been running for miles and miles.

"But Emily's a gourmet cook. She'll spoil that man to death." Mother lifted the platter, examined it, added more lettuce leaves and carried it to the refrigerator. "Your father will work till the last rose has been dug. He says it's going to rain and he's very anxious to get some new fertilizer into the ground first. Let's sit on the porch a few minutes, dear. I want to hear all about your day. Do you think it's going to be very hard? Taking care of Gino, I mean."

They went to the porch and sat down.

"I'm going to dote on it, Mother. He's the darlingest little thing. I'm going to teach him as much English as I can. It must be dreadful not to understand what people are saying. He chatters ribbons of Italian. Maybe he can teach me some. I think his grandfather likes me. I . . . I *think* he does."

"Debbie dear, of course he does. How could he help it? It's pretty wonderful for him to have you take the boy off his hands every afternoon. Listen, I have an idea. Wouldn't you like to invite Alec Belmont to dinner Friday night? Wouldn't that be a nice gesture after his helping you with the mirror? Emily agrees with me that—"

"Mother!" Debbie's cry was a mixture of horror and delight. She couldn't imagine inviting Alec to dinner. He'd think her stark mad. Pushy. Eager. Infantile. Nonetheless it was a delectable if horrifying idea.

"You needn't sound so scandalized, dear," Mother laughed. "Emily and I thought as long as we'd be having a particularly good dinner it might be opportune to ask him. Don't give it another thought. Forgive us for seeming to run your life." Mother got up and went into the house.

Wind stirred the honeysuckle and spread its perfume on the quiet evening air. Birds chirped sleepily in the trees. A power mower whirred somewhere. There was the familiar clackety clack of roller skates. The sounds and the smells of summer were all dear to Debbie's heart. She got up rather suddenly and followed her mother into the kitchen.

"I didn't mean to yell at you like that, Mother." Debbie leaned against her. "You never seem to run my life. I didn't mean that at all. It's just that Alec would think. . . . Oh, I don't know. I'd love to," she added, looking out the window, not meeting her mother's interested eyes.

"Think it over, dear, and let me know. Aunt Em, too, of course, as she's bringing the meal. Will you call your father?"

"Cranberries! I forgot. I was supposed to call him when I got out of the bathroom." Debbie flew to the front door.

Dad was on his way to the house, still whistling that tuneless air between his teeth, swinging a basket of tools and a bag of fertilizer with an obvious air of satisfaction.

"You're right about the rain," he said, gazing at the sky. He handed her the basket, stripped off his work gloves and dropped them into it. "Take it to the basement, will you, dear? I'll get a bath."

"What *is* this stuff? It smells perfectly horrible! Hurry, Dad, will you? I forgot to call you."

As he went down the hall, he shook his head saying, "Debbie, Debbie, Debbie."

He might as well have said, *When will you ever grow up?*

Holding her breath, she closed the heavy paper bag of fertilizer and tied the string tightly around it. Flying to the basement, she exhaled with a loud "Whew!"

"Just the same," Mother smiled as Debbie returned to the kitchen, "it does wonders for the roses. Don't forget that."

As she sat down at the table, Debbie realized that if her parents had the faintest notion how tired she was, they wouldn't let her continue the job. It was in that moment that she decided not to tell any of the Muscatels about it. Not until after the first week. When she was sure of permission to go on, it would be plenty of time to let the others know.

Dad, looking clean, cool, and damp about the head, seemed to have an unusually good appetite.

Debbie had none. Afraid of revealing her excessive fatigue, she forced herself to eat a little. She complimented Mother on the potato salad.

"It had better be good," Mother said, smiling. "It's my sole reason for being president of the Auxiliary, you know."

Dad helped himself to more. "We got a shipment of little cars today," he said. "Automobiles, I mean. One of them is damaged and has some of the paint scraped off. It's too bad. They're very expensive. Even so, we sold two this afternoon. Fantastic, the money people spend on things."

"Dad," Debbie said eagerly, "do you suppose there's any chance of getting it for Gino? Cheap?"

"I don't know, dear, but I'll be glad to find out. It needs repairs and a coat of paint. I'll inquire in the morning. Deb'rah," he patted Mother's hand, "this salad *is* unusually good."

"That's because you have a sense of accomplishment about your roses. Think we'll have lots this year?" Mother poured herself a second glass of tea and held the pitcher up toward Dad.

Holding his glass to be filled, he said, "They look fine so far. I hope the rain in the air will materialize. They need it. Debbie, you're not eating much."

She smiled at him and said, "Aren't you wild to meet Aunt Em's fiancé?" It was important to keep her parents' attention away from herself.

"He sounds splendid," Dad said. "Emily stopped by the store for a ball of twine and told me more about him. Yes, I'm very eager to meet him. She certainly seems happy. Blissfully happy. Dear girl. She deserves the best. No doubt about that."

"She told me not to expect an Adonis," Mother said.

"Oh, I hope he's tall and, well, if not handsome, at least distinguished looking," Debbie said. "It would be a tragedy for Aunt Em to marry a homely man, wouldn't it?"

"Naturally, you can't expect another bee-utiful job like your father to join the ranks of the Robynes," Dad teased. "That would be too much like cornering the market on looks."

"George, you idiot!" Mother laughed. Her eyes told him

that as far as she was concerned, she had the prize. "I hope she'll be as happy as I am."

"You are bee-utiful in an older sort of way," Debbie nodded. "Even if you weren't, we'd love and adore you; wouldn't we, Mother?"

They laughed as though thoroughly amused.

"Could I . . . ?" Abruptly, Debbie stopped talking. She had been on the point of asking if she could postpone washing the dishes until morning. They would ask why and she could not, would not tell them. "Could I have half a glass of tea?"

The rain had started by the time she went to bed. A gentle rain, perfect for the roses. However, it failed to cool the air. Debbie pulled a sheet half over her and went to sleep the second her head made its nest in her pillow.

She dreamed that she and Alec were walking through a cool starlit forest hand in hand. From the treetops came strains of lilting melody which set their feet to dancing— only they didn't dance, just walked in time with the music. The forest floor was covered with flowers of all colors and sizes, each with a fragrance sweeter than the last. They heard the sound of water and hurried to find its source. When they came upon a narrow rushing stream between banks of ferns and lilies, Alec begged Debbie to sit down. He wanted to make a wreath of flowers for her hair. Like a crown. She longed to stay with him beside the stream but suddenly it appeared swollen, threatening to overflow its banks. And the sound of the water was no longer delicious. It was frightening. Terrifying. . . .

She woke up abruptly, shaking with fear. And with cold. The air had chilled. It was raining in perfect torrents and the wind blew terribly hard.

Debbie pulled up the soft white blanket Aunt Em had given her for Christmas. Without getting out of bed and closing her windows, she went back to sleep, hoping in vain to prolong the dream of Alec.

When she opened her eyes in the morning, a sorry sight greeted her. The dotted swiss curtains hung limp and bedraggled. Soaked. Water stood in pools on the floor under both windows. Even the end of the blue rag rug was dark and wet. She dashed to the bathroom for towels and tried to mop up the floor. The water had stood so long it left great ugly light spots even after the boards had been wiped dry. Dad would scold her. Mother would have to wash and iron the curtains. . . .

"Debbie?" Mother called and knocked on the door.

"Yes, Mother? I'm trying to mop up the rain. It got all over everything. Must have been a cloudburst. Come in!"

"Didn't you close your windows? But of course not, or there wouldn't be this . . . oh, Debbie! Just look at the floor! And the curtains . . . even the rug!" Mother chewed her lips in an apparent effort at control. The next moment she left the room quickly, calling over her shoulder, "Hurry and get dressed or you'll be late to school. You overslept."

"You'd have overslept, too, if you'd been as hurt and tired as I was." But the words stayed in Debbie's mind. She hurried frantically. Dad didn't tolerate her being tardy to meals. She really should have gotten up in time to set the table for breakfast.

When she went into the kitchen, she found Mother and Dad already seated.

"I'm sorry to be late," she said, slipping into her chair and trying to smile.

"Mother tells me that you failed to close your windows during the storm," Dad said in his flat voice of disapproval. "And it rained all over the curtains and the floor and. . . . Did you wake up, Debbie? Or," he leaned toward her, his brown eyes half-closed, "were you so exhausted after your first session with Gino that you didn't hear the rain?"

He mustn't think that! "Oh, I woke up, Dad. I heard the rain and that tearing wind. I really did hear it. I was so cold. So terribly cold. I pulled up my blanket just for a minute before getting up and . . . well, I went right back to sleep. The room's a mess. I'm afraid the floor will have to be waxed or varnished or whatever is done to floors. And, Mother, I'm sorry, but you'll have to wash—"

"Your mother will have to wash nothing." Dad's voice had turned to ice. "You will launder your own curtains and iron them. As to the floor, perhaps you can repair that, too."

"Cranberries, Dad! I don't know anything about refinishing floors!"

"Perhaps it's time you learned." He drank half a cup of coffee.

She was afraid to look at him. Or at Mother. Her eyes strayed around the kitchen. Even in her anxiety, she was conscious of the care and thought expended upon this room, Mother's favorite in the house. The floor was gray tile, the warm gray of summer clouds. Dad had painted the chairs yellow and Mother had made ruffled curtains the same shade. Pots of small-leafed ivy were on either side of the sink in armed metal brackets which, Dad said, had held oil lamps in some old house in the country. The effect was pleasing. Restful.

There was no sound except the quiet hum of the refrigerator in the corner.

Dad set his cup down, wiped his mouth on a yellow checked napkin and gave his undivided attention to Debbie. He cocked his white head and held her eyes with his. "It's just such a circumstance as this that makes us doubt your dependability, Debbie. It seems to us that a girl irresponsible enough to let rain practically swamp her room is not fit to take care of a three-year-old boy. Not responsible enough. Not—"

A rush of panic poured through her. "Please, Dad! Please let me go on. I—I've just got to. I'll take care of my room. I'll find out what to do to the floors and I'll wash and iron the curtains over the weekend. Mother," Debbie turned to her, "won't you give me another chance? It's not taking care of Gino that's so hard. Oh, it's hard enough, in a way. But something that happened at school . . . that's what mowed me down. I'm honestly not quite as careless as you and Dad think. You'll let me keep the job? Oh, you must! You've got to! Dad, you know about floors. Will you get what I need at the store? I'll pay for it. Not that I know just how at the moment," she tossed a dazzling smile between them. "But I'll find a way. You'll see. What's the verdict of you two bee-utiful people?"

"None of your blandishments," Dad said.

But she saw the corners of his lips quiver and took heart.

"What say, Deb'rah?"

"Oh, yes, George. She wants to prove something to herself. And to us. Besides"—Mother blushed—"I can't bear to part with that exquisite mirror." She gave him her most appealing smile.

"Shall we try it for another week?" Dad asked.

"No," Debbie said emphatically. "We shan't try it for another week. I've got a job and, by cranberry, I'm going to hold onto it. I'll show you. I'll show you both. I'll prove . . . oh, what it is you want me to prove!" She took a piece of toast and stood up. "I drank my orange juice and this is all I want. I'll get back to normal pretty soon. 'Bye, I've got to tear!" She kissed them both, received an affectionate spank from Dad and ran to her room for books and purse.

It was more important than ever to prove her maturity. Debbie acknowledged this. It frightened her.

14

From Dream to Nightmare

The next afternoon found Debbie in a dream of delight as Alec drove her and Gino to his grandfather's farm. She decided that after all she would invite him to Aunt Em's dinner.

"What a perfectly bee-utiful place, Alec," she said, unconsciously lowering her voice.

They drove down a lengthy avenue of old oak trees and through a gate open in a high white fence. The columned house stood stately as a duchess on a velvet lawn.

"What's that marvelous smell? Locusts?"

"There's a grove back of the house." Alec nodded. "I hope Gino won't be afraid to get on a horse."

"Horse!" he cried unexpectedly. "Horse, horse, horse!" His black eyes glittered, and he rocked with laughter.

"You're a pretty smart kid," Alec said. And to Debbie, "You'd almost think he knew what he was talking about. He's cute, all right. I don't blame you for being crazy about him, brown-eyes."

She nodded and looked around her as Alec stopped the car under the *porte cochere*.

The house was magnificent. Built of brick, painted white, it was at least sixty feet across the front with wide porches shaded by a sloping roof with dormer windows. There were several smaller brick buildings. Countless old shade trees laid purple shadows on the grass. There was the impression of quiet and peace. A sense of opulence pervaded everything.

Carlotta would lose her mind over this place. Carlotta! She had been absent today and Debbie had been spared another lecture.

"Well, come on, let's get out and look around," Alec said.

"I've been looking. It's pretty fabulous." Over the high fence around the enclosure in which the house stood, fruit trees dropped branches heavy with budding bloom. In one corner toward the back, gardens had been cultivated and the young green of flowers grew in the rich earth. A trembling golden light was over all. "It's like a fairyland," Debbie said very softly.

Alec laughed. "It's just a farm, brown-eyes. Let's go back to the stables. There, through that gate. Down in that pasture that you can see through the fence are the black Angus. Cows. Say cow, Gino!" He scooped Gino up into his arms.

Gino twisted about, laughing.

"Go on, darling, say cow," Debbie begged.

"Cow, cow, cow!"

"He's learning awfully fast—" Alec said.

"Cow, cow, cow!" Gino shouted. "Debbie, Debbie. . . ."

"Hey, fella, stop your jumping. I can't hold onto you when you bounce like that!" Alec laughed and squeezed him hard.

"Isn't he adorable? Don't you think he is, Alec?" It was important to Debbie that he agree with her.

"Sure is. You want to get on a horse, Gino? I know you do."

"Oh, Alec, do you think he should? He's so little and not being quite able to walk. . . . He's only taken a couple of steps so far."

"I don't want him to walk on the horse! I want him to ride one. Of course he should. Grandpa put me on horseback long before I could take a step. Gino'll love it. I can bet on that."

She wasn't at all sure he would love it. Even if he did, was it safe? He had probably never been near a horse before and might be terrified.

They went to the stables, two long low buildings with gabled roofs. Inside the first, it seemed dark after the brilliant out-of-doors. There was the smell of ammonia and leather, and the indescribable sound of horses moving in stalls, switching their tails and neighing in whispers.

A tall lanky redheaded boy appeared out of the shadows. He was eating an apple. "Howdy, Alec," he said with a wide grin. "Want to ride Christmas?"

"No, Speed. I want the boy to ride. Better let him have Dawn. She's the gentlest. Lead her out, h'm? No saddle. Just put a folded blanket on her. And a bridle."

"Cute little old boy," he said. "Belong to you, Alec?" The cackle of laughter which followed told Debbie that he was teasing.

"This is Miss Debbie Robyne, Speed. We'll get her up on Dawn after the boy rides."

None of that jazz for me, she thought, shivering.

"Come along, let's have a look at the cattle while Speed gets the horse ready. Toledo! That locust smell is strong. Sort of sickening. Smothers any other blossoms." Alec made a face.

The trees were filled with bees buzzing like machinery.

Gino was fairly palpitating with excitement. In Alec's arms he turned and twisted, jumped and leaped until Debbie was afraid he would fall. However, Alec's arms were strong and he seemed to be holding onto his burden plenty tight.

So concerned was she that she did not see an oriole fly from a nearby tree to balance on the tip of a branch a few feet away. But she knew when it showered them with deep, clear song. She stopped quite still to listen, hearing Gino's laughter in the beauty of the sound.

Debbie wanted more than anything to prolong this golden hour here on the meadow path, watching the cattle grazing peacefully, hearing the old trees chanting overhead and the quiet splashing of a brook making a little waterfall over rocks. She pulled a pale pink wild flower like a star and held it to her lips.

Alec reached over, took the blossom and tucked it in her hair. He shook his head, smiling crookedly, his lean face close to hers. "It's not right," he said. "You ought to have big bright flowers to carry out the motif of your dark hair and eyes."

Debbie was hurt. She would much prefer to resemble a pale pink star.

"You look like a girl who'd love camping," he continued.

"But I'll bet you've never spent a single night in the woods."

"Horse!" Gino shouted, pointing to a black Angus cow. Debbie and Alec laughed.

"I used to when I was a kid, with the Girl Scouts, but I wasn't too hopped up about it."

"For my money, nothing can touch the woods very early in the morning. Couple of weeks ago, Carl and I camped overnight on the Meramec River. It poured during the night but in the morning. . . ." Alec shook his head and a band of sunlight streaked across his blond hair. "It was really something. All the trees and bushes glittered with big drops like jewels. And the little streams all swollen with rain rushed between the trees with a sound like—like the way he laughs." He ducked his head to touch the dark one of the boy in his arms.

"Oh, Alec," Debbie whispered breathlessly, deeply moved. Her heart beat wildly. Along with everything else desirable, he was a poet.

"Look at the black Angus shine in the sun," he said abruptly. "Magnificent! Worth plenty, too."

At that moment, Speed called that Dawn was ready.

They hurried back to the stable yard where a totally white mare stood bridled and blanketed in scarlet.

What a picture! But Debbie didn't say it aloud. She was instantly concerned about Gino's getting aboard such a tall animal. He would be terribly high in the air.

With no ado, Alec lifted the boy onto the horse's back and motioned Speed to hand him the bridle.

Debbie held her breath in an agony of apprehension.

"Don't look so panicked." Alec shook her arm. "Dawn's

very gentle. Dozens of kids have learned to ride on her back. She won't run with Gino."

"For the love of cranberries, I should hope not!" Debbie stole a fearful look at the boy and couldn't help laughing.

He looked as though he belonged exactly where he was at the moment. He sat very straight, holding the bridle in both little hands and beaming more brightly than the sun.

Alec clucked. Dawn turned her head, looked at him and started to walk away.

"Oh, no, don't let him go without you, Alec!"

"Good night, brown-eyes, he's okay. Look at him! He's perfectly at home on horseback. Not the least bit scared. If that's not one to report!" Alec doubled over, laughing. "I thought he'd like it, but blamed if I expected him to ride like a veteran. He sits a horse just about perfectly. We've never seen one like that, Speed!"

Speed removed a soiled, white visored cap and scratched his flaming short hair. "Beats me, Alec," he said, restoring the cap. "Sure beats me."

"But he's my responsibility," Debbie said. "I can't let him go off that way on that great tall animal! Where's he going?"

"Dawn will walk up to the *porte cochere,* turn around and walk slowly back. It's a regular routine with her. That's why I chose her for Gino. I don't want him to be hurt any more than you do."

"Don't you think I'd better go along, too?" Debbie rubbed her hands together nervously. The palms were wet.

"You surprise me, brown-eyes. You do for sure." Alec

scowled and looked cross. "When you ride, you'll see how gentle she happens to be."

"When I get aboard, it'll be a freezing day in summer." But her words made no more sound than that made by the wild flower falling from her hair. "Speed," she said aloud, "won't you go with him?"

"He'd spoil Gino's fun!" Alec cried. "Don't be silly! He's having the time of his life and he's perfectly safe. I can guarantee it. Go on back to your whittling, Speed."

Glancing from Alec to Debbie and back, shaking his head, Speed finally obeyed Alec.

"You'll see I'm right, so forget it," Alec said, taking her arm. "Speed's mother is Grandpa's cook and always has something good to eat. Let's tackle her in the kitchen."

"Go in the house while Gino's out here on that horse?" she cried. "Not in a thousand years. We'll wait for him."

With a long-drawn sigh, Alec sat down on a green-painted bench and resignedly patted the place beside him.

"I can't sit down. I just can't. I'm too worried. . . ."

"Have a look. She's turning around and coming back. The kid is the picture of joy if ever I saw one. He's one big grin from ear to ear." Alec clapped his hands in delight.

Relieved beyond measure, Debbie sat down on the very edge of the bench.

A moment later, in spite of the fact that Gino made it amply clear that he objected, Alec pulled him off the horse.

Before Debbie had time to protest, Alec then lifted her to Dawn's back and gave a loud cluck. Once again the horse walked toward the house.

For a moment, Debbie was paralyzed. Then, like a dark

tide, rushed the same sensation as that in her dream of looking down into that night-black apartment court. Determined not to let Alec suspect her panic, she managed to still the scream which she seemed actually to hear in her throat. It was impossible to control the sickness which pervaded her. Everything around her quivered with light and she discerned the house, the high fence and the trees through a kind of haze. She was almost blind with terror. Determined not to, she nonetheless screamed—an involuntary sound of sheer panic. It startled Dawn and she threw her head back wildly and began to run. The scream seemed to float and tremble in the air all around.

Alec shouted, "Whoa, Dawn, whoa!"

The obedient animal stopped at once and turned an inquiring head toward him.

"Take me down! Oh, Alec, take me down!" Debbie screamed.

After what seemed a lifetime, he lifted her from the horse. In truth, Debbie practically fell into his raised arms, limp and terrified.

Alec was amused. His eyes danced, wickedly bright and blue. His mouth was set for laughter. "Gino will have the laugh on you, brown-eyes," he teased, and gave her a little shake. "Being afraid of that gentle animal. Why, *he* rode her with a broad grin."

He didn't really laugh aloud at her, but she was sure that he wanted to. Feeling about him as she did, his teasing hurt. He wouldn't act that way if he was at all interested in her. Rather, he would be concerned and sorry that he had arbitrarily set her on that horse. Why should he be interested in her kind of girl when Carlotta's kind was so close by? Even a passing thought of Carlotta had the power to sadden Debbie. She was suddenly frightfully depressed. So many things troubled her.

"Now, we'll tackle Speed's mother for something good to eat and a cool drink," Alec announced.

"If you like. I'll just sit here on this bench. I'm not hungry."

"I'll bet Gino is!" Alec picked him up and held him high in the air. "You'll have some cookies, fella!"

"Cooky, cooky, cooky!" Gino laughed and held out his arms to Debbie.

She couldn't resist him and got up and accompanied him and Alec into the house.

The kitchen was like a picture in *House Beautiful*. Not a stainless steel and gleaming tile affair, but a huge room with a fireplace, a room in which Debbie felt she could stay for the rest of her life, happily. The floor was of dark and shining brick. All cabinets were polished walnut. Three walls combined these materials and against them hung copper pots and molds. The third wall was the color of rich cream and on it hung a picture of the house made entirely of bits of white and colored material sewn onto a cloth background of leaf green.

"This is the most beautiful room I ever saw," Debbie said softly. "Why, your whole entire life could be lived right here." Her voice was hushed, her brown eyes almost black.

"You like it, dear?" a woman's voice asked.

Debbie turned and saw Speed's mother. "I know you're

Speed's mother because of your hair," she said. "Oh, don't you just adore working in this room?"

Alec and the woman laughed indulgently.

"I told you Lena'd have something good for us," Alec said, indicating a silver tray of cakes and tall iced drinks. "Skip the dining room, Lena. We'll sit right here at the kitchen table."

Gino was actually walking around the room with his hands locked behind him inspecting everything but touching nothing.

"Lena, this is Debbie Robyne," Alec said. "And the boy's name is Gino. Sit down, Debbie, and absorb a little nourishment. Gino won't need urging. He's taken plenty more than two steps in here!"

"May I hold the boy on my lap, Alec?" Lena asked, following Gino with interested eyes.

They sat down. The thought crossed Debbie's mind that Alec wouldn't have settled for a kitchen snack if Carlotta had been his guest. Not that Debbie objected to eating in the kitchen—she loved it. But she resented the thought that Alec wasn't giving her as much house as he would have given Carlotta. Then, abruptly, she scolded herself for thinking like a child. How did she know the way Alec felt? Maybe he preferred the kitchen.

Anyhow, she was glad that she hadn't invited him to dinner.

"Your grandpa's showing the black Angus at the Fair," Lena was saying. "And he said I could enter my peach conserve if I liked."

"You'll win a blue ribbon, sure," Alec said, pushing a

plate of little cakes toward Debbie. "The Jefferson County Fair," he said. "Coming soon."

Ordinarily wild about going to the Fair, Debbie was too concerned with her own secret thoughts to pay attention to the discussion between Alec and Lena. The afternoon, begun on such a high note, was ending considerably further down the scale.

15

Perfect Performances

"Gino! Gino, come back here, you little imp!" Smiling, Debbie ran after him as he took off across the Karidale Boulevard sidewalk toward the street. Since his surprising parade about the Belmont kitchen, he had never been still. She scooped him up and kissed his warm, flushed cheek. "What's the idea of heading for all the traffic, angel?"

He was heavy to lift; heavier to hold. Even in her arms, he didn't stop moving. She decided that he was the closest thing to perpetual motion she had ever seen. She put him down and held his hand tightly within her own.

It was another hot afternoon. Gino was scantily clad in a brilliant yellow short-sleeved shirt and brief pants. He looked adorable and completely Italian. If only she could find a vendor with scarlet balloons. . . .

She imagined Gino strolling along the shore of the blue, blue Mediterranean while gondolas and starched white yachts supplied a fitting background. A handsome dark Italian boy approached and said softly, "Beautiful *bambino*. Yours?" Debbie laughed, realizing that she had placed herself as well as Gino on that magic shore.

"Better keep my mind on my job," she whispered, "or you will be making your escape sure enough."

Yesterday, Mr. Fieldson had given her a dime for ice cream. Today, to his amazement and Debbie's, Gino had approached with his hand outstretched, saying, "Cream, cream, cream."

They had gone into a small drugstore on a side street and sat on high stools at the fountain. She had watched the boy devour every whisper of ice cream. It had probably not occurred to old Mr. Fieldson that she too might enjoy some. Or, if he thought of it, he would take it for granted that she would buy it. Not while they were on this wretched budget. There were no extra dimes for anybody.

The boy at the fountain had been awfully nice. He had offered her a spoon, ducking his head toward Gino's dish of ice cream, much as to say, "Go ahead, share it with the kid."

She had refused but appreciated the thoughtful gesture. Today she returned. They went through the same routine.

"It's one way to keep him quiet," Debbie said.

"Your little brother?"

She shook her head. "I just take care of him, afternoons. He's darling, isn't he?" She poked a spoon full of ice cream between Gino's smiling lips.

"You better sit still, kid. You're gonna take a tumble off that high stool if you ain't careful."

"I don't believe he'll fall," Debbie said. "You should see the way he sits on a horse."

At that moment with no warning, Gino simply threw himself toward her. Only by the greatest imaginable luck and speed was she able to drop the spoon and catch him.

The fountain boy whistled. "Sa-ay! What kind of trapeze artist do you think you are, bub? You could get hurt bad doing stunts like that. You sure moved fast to catch him," he added with an admiring look at Debbie.

"One thing for sure!" She laughed breathlessly. "He keeps me one hundred percent alert. Gino," she said then, frowning at him and being very serious, "you must never do that again. No, no, no." She shook her head.

"No, no, no!" He mimicked word and gesture.

"Whadda you know?" The fountain boy wiped off the counter with a dingy wet rag. "Don't you want a glass of water or something, miss?"

"Thanks just the same." She wiped Gino's ice-creamy lips with a paper napkin, crumpled it into his empty glass cup, and slid to the floor. "Come on, darling."

"Watch it! He's going into his trapeze stunt again!"

"Oh, no, you're not, my angel." She grabbed Gino and stood him on the floor.

Quick as a smile he scampered to a circular rack of paperback books and gave it a violent spin, laughing and jumping and throwing himself from side to side.

"Cranberries," Debbie sighed. "You're quite a fistful. Come on outside before you wreck the place."

"See you!" the fountain boy called. "And keep your eyes open. The kid's got springs instead of bones."

Debbie, returning him to his grandfather, fully agreed. She hoped, a trifle desperately, that Gino wouldn't get any peppier. Of course she wanted him to be healthy and strong. And she was pleased by his rosy color. But there was a limit to what she could control, and Gino had almost reached it.

On the way home she passed the Karidale Bakery. The front door was open. The fragrance of fresh-baked bread and cake struck her like a blow. At a table in the front of the shop, two women were drinking iced tea and eating little frosted cakes.

A bit unsteady from fatigue and hunger, Debbie hurried by, thinking of Lena and the delectable cakes and drinks she had prepared. Imagine! Alec was probably accustomed to that sort of service every day of his life. Oh, well, Mother was a magnif cook, and the Robyne kitchen was a cozy, good-smelling place to eat in. She didn't need a fine, big house and uniformed maid to make her happy. If only she and Carlotta were as close. . . . She had been absent again today and the Muscatels wondered why. Carlotta. Golden Girl. Until recently the thought of her had been a joy. Now it brought only pain. How would Carlotta act the next time they met? It was an anxious question to which there was as yet no answer.

As she covered the last two blocks, Debbie's only thought was of a long sudsy bath and a cool, cool shower. One thing to be grateful for was that no matter how Gino wore her out she had been able so far to hide it from Mother and Dad.

Mother met her at the front door with news.

"Surprise, surprise!" she called, holding the screen door open. "Cynthia's coming to supper!"

Without speaking, Debbie went into the house and closed the door.

"I knew you'd be glad to see her. The poor girl has called so many times. She misses you so, dear. She has an awfully hard time, really. And she never complains. As a matter of fact, she wanted you to have supper with her. A neighbor is bringing her mother's meal in and will spend the evening with Mrs. Maddern. I thought you might be tired and rather have Cynthia here. She was delighted to accept. You see, Emily, dear girl, came by with half an elegant cake and a bowl of salad."

"Oh, Mother." Debbie gave her a quick hug. "Thanks. I'll get a bath before Dad comes. Okay?"

"Take your time, dear. Everything's under control," Mother called as Debbie went down the hall to her room.

As she bathed and dressed, she wondered how Alec would react to their way of life. He might feel sorry for them, or be amused, or scornful. Somehow, Debbie didn't believe that. He might even enjoy the simplicity. Well, she was not about to find out. She had not invited him to Aunt Em's dinner.

Cynthia arrived a few minutes before Debbie was dressed.

"Be there in a sec!" she called, wondering if she could make it through the evening without falling apart. She had never dreamed that taking care of a lively three-year-old could be so tiring. *Be honest; you know it's the emotional strain that's bugging you the most.* "Stay in the living room, Cyn, it's cooler in there." A moment later she said, "Cyn! You look adorable!"

"Mother made it. All by hand. Imagine! Wasn't it darling of her? Look at the tiny stitches. She got our neighbor to buy the material and a pattern, and she cut it out, too. But Mother did every bit of the sewing. It's a lovely shade of green, isn't it?"

"You're a lovely shade of you," Debbie said quietly, gladder to see Cynthia than ever before. Suddenly, looking into her gray eyes so dark and bright with affection and pleasure, Debbie had a brainstorm. It spun wild and gay from the intrigue in her head. "How's about seeing if Ring can come to supper?"

Color flooded Cynthia's face and her lips parted in a lovely smile.

"You'd go for that, wouldn't you, Cyn? If Mother says it's okay?"

The bright head nodded enthusiastically.

Debbie ran to the kitchen. "Will Aunt Em's cake and salad stretch?" she asked her mother. Then she whispered softly, "Cyn's got a thing for Ring Putnam and I thought it would be fun to ask him. If you don't mind."

"Why, what an excellent idea! By all means call him. I'll set another place. We're having supper on the porch. Tell him about six thirty. That will give your father some time to bathe."

Debbie stood in deep thought for a moment, then said, hoping to further her already spinning intrigue, "Could you and Dad and I go to Aunt Em's Saturday night? To meet her fiancé?" She had managed to put Ring off for last Saturday but. . . .

"He's out of town, dear, or we'd have met him before now." Mother gave Debbie a long, speculative look and added, "But there's no reason why we couldn't go to see Emily."

"The three of us?"

Mother nodded. "Yes, of course."

Debbie called, "Look up Ring's number, will you, Cyn? It's all set." And to Mother, "What sort of meat are we having?"

"You wait and see, dear. I've fixed a casserole of everything unanchored and it's real good. Cheese and crumbs on top."

"You're a living wonder!" Smiling confidently, Debbie went to call Ring.

He accepted with alacrity and arrived before Dad had finished dressing.

Debbie opened the door and said very quietly, "I'm so glad you could come, Ring. But I have to tell you, I can't go to the movies with you this Saturday, either. My Aunt Emily Robyne's engaged and we're all going to her apartment. It—it's important, you see." Debbie felt enormously clever to have taken such good care of the situation. Now, perhaps he would invite Cynthia to the movies.

He started to say something when he caught sight of Cynthia coming down the hall. "What do you know!" he said as if surprised and, Debbie hoped, pleased. "The atomic redhead. Hi!"

"Hi." That was all Cynthia said. Just "Hi." But the way she looked and the sudden lift of her lovely eyes, the tilt of her head gave as warm a welcome as anybody could possibly hope for.

Debbie thought that the evening was off to a good start.

"Something smells wonderful," Ring said when they all went to the porch. "And," he added with a smile, "I don't mean the honeysuckle."

He seemed perfectly relaxed and at home. He held Mother's chair, and he bowed his dark head when Dad said grace. Debbie saw that they both liked him.

She had arranged for Cynthia to sit opposite Ring so that he could see what a real doll she was. She said very little at first. Ring had lost every vestige of his former shyness and told about the college he planned to attend in northern Michigan, and how he had discovered it when he and his uncle had taken a fishing trip to Isle Royale.

"Where is Isle Royale?" Cynthia asked the question softly and yet managed to convey the impression that she was deeply interested.

"In Lake Superior. It's a national park. We drove to Houghton up on the Keweenaw Peninsula and took the Ranger Third, a swell Government passenger boat. My grandparents used to own a summer cabin, so Uncle's been there lots of times. They sold to the Government when the island was taken over for a national park. It's a real wilderness. Beautiful and wild as all get out. Moose, wolves, coyotes. . . ."

"But about the college, Ring?" Dad said, smiling.

"Michigan College of Mines and Technology. Swell engineering school. It's in Houghton."

"Sounds awfully far away," Cynthia said, very low.

"My uncle's going to let me have my own car and I'll be driving back for holidays and stuff like that. I don't know what this is"—he gave Mother a wide smile—"but it sure is good!"

"My wife has a brown thumb," Dad said proudly. "She can assemble the weirdest assortment of leftovers and come up with delicious things floating in rich brown gravy. I've always been glad I married a girl who knows what to do with food. It's mighty important."

"Have some more, Ring," Mother said, pleased and letting him know it. "There's loads here."

"You bet I will. Thanks." He passed his plate and won her admiration forever.

Debbie yawned and made quite a point of excusing it.

"Everything is marvelous, Mrs. Robyne," Cynthia said. "I'm so glad I came here instead of Debbie's having supper with me. It's a treat to eat out here where you can see the birds and smell the honeysuckle. If I ever have a home of my own, I hope I can have a big porch where we can have our meals in good weather. It's perfectly lovely."

Cynthia's voice was one of her best features. It was low and bell-clear with an unmistakable cadence. If you heard it once, Debbie was thinking, you'd recognize it anywhere in the world.

"Mr. Robyne's sister made the salad and the cake," Mother said as she and Debbie cleared the table. "She says she's never made this kind of cake before but it certainly looks elegant."

"I'll say it does," Ring said when it appeared in thick slices. "What kind is it, Mrs. Robyne?"

Debbie was delighted by his interest in food, and she could have kissed Dad for emphasizing the importance of being a good cook.

"I haven't the foggiest notion, Ring," Mother said.

Cynthia tasted hers. "Burnt sugar with caramel frosting," she said. "But it's more than that. I mean there's something between the layers in this thick yummy filling. . . ."

The others waited as if upon some decision of great moment.

"I know!" Cynthia cried after a moment more of tasting. "English walnuts and candied orange peel. I've never eaten anything as good in my life!"

"You're sure?" Ring asked, his intensely clear eyes registering pleasure. "I mean that it's walnuts and . . . and that other stuff?"

"Cyn's a natural cook," Debbie said. "She and Mother and Aunt Em. They're absolutely tops." She stifled another yawn with the fingers of both hands. "Sorry," she said with a feeling of the most mischievous delight.

She was not faking fatigue, but she was purposely calling attention to it. When she caught Dad's worried eyes upon her she decided to play it low until he and Mother had gone to the meeting at church.

After their departure, Cynthia suggested sitting on the porch.

Debbie wanted to, but she was afraid the darkness would hide her act.

It was not hidden in the lighted living room. She saw to her keen satisfaction that the quieter and droopier she grew, the more Cynthia took over. Ring was frankly more and more interested in her.

About an hour later, he said with a semblance of his old timidity, "You seem pretty beat, Debbie; maybe Cynthia and I had better scram and let you get to bed. I guess that little Italian kid keeps you humping."

"That he does. He's plenty strenuous. I don't want to be

rude, kids, but. . . ." Her words were effectively blotted out by a yawn.

She almost laughed aloud at their expressions of joy. She wondered a bit giddily if even Aunt Em could have achieved a more outstanding success in one evening.

16

Terrifying Moment

One afternoon, Debbie was in the bed-sitting room buttoning a scarlet sweater over Gino's chest when old Mr. Fieldson approached.

His air of timidity was totally unfamiliar and captured her immediate attention. "Child," he said, "you do me a big favor, huh?"

"If I can, Mr. Fieldson, sure." She was in the mood for doing favors. Cynthia had told her that she and Ring were going to the movies Saturday night. As a result, Debbie felt the stirring of confidence in herself. "While Gino and I are out walking?" she asked.

He held his chin and regarded her steadily for a moment. "Not while you're out, Debbie. No. I'd like for you to stay in." His rough black head was thrown back, his eyes half-closed. "I got to go downtown on business. It's very urgent or I wouldn't ask you. You'll watch shop for me? You and the boy?"

"I'd be glad to. It might be fun. But what if a customer should come?" The possibility made her uneasy. She wouldn't have the faintest idea how to handle the situation.

"Mrs. Ermine may stop by to look at her tea caddy and if anybody else comes. . . ." He smiled broadly and his face twinkled the way Gino's did. "If another customer shows up . . . *sell* something!"

"Oh, Mr. Fieldson, I'm no salesgirl." She laughed. She allowed herself to toy briefly with the idea of selling. She had listened to the old man and his customers, and had been impressed by his ability to allow the buyer literally to talk himself into thinking he had secured a rare bargain. Debbie seriously doubted her ability to emulate the old man, though she would love to handle the beautiful antiques.

"I'll show you where the key to the cabinet hangs. Be sure to keep it locked, Debbie. You know it's filled with my most valuable items."

Holding Gino's hand, she followed Mr. Fieldson's slightly waddling gait into the shop and to the hiding-place for the key. Nodding when he indicated the key, she secretly admitted to being nervous. She had a hunch that this could be some sort of a test for her. Hoping for an uninterrupted afternoon, she agreed to stay inside with Gino, and to do her best.

"I'm not sure you couldn't sell, Debbie. But I'll get back as soon as possible. Won't be over an hour; I promise. And thank you, child." The old man hurried away, hatless. His fat legs and little feet made remarkable speed.

"Well, sugar-shoes," Debbie hugged Gino. "It's up to you and me for a while." She had grown fonder and fonder of the boy. He was the most responsive little thing. He seemed in some mysterious way to understand practically everything she said. And when he looked at her with those great laughing black eyes and held up his arms, she was lost. How dreadfully she was going to miss him this summer! She pushed the thought away.

"Cream, Debbie?" He patted her cheek. Suddenly his laughter fell in a bright torrent, bouncing around the shop sweet as music.

"Oh, Gino, not today, angel. Unless your grandpa comes back in time for us to go to the drugstore. Any cookies left?"

"Cooky," he said, standing straight with his feet wide apart like a little man. "Gino have cooky." He took her hand and led her to the kitchen where a paper sack of cookies stood open on the table. He reached for it but couldn't quite make contact. He turned to her with his dazzling smile. "Cooky, Debbie!"

She gave him one. He took a bite and said, "Cooky for Debbie."

"That's not a bad idea." She laughed and helped herself. Munching the cooky, she said, "Gino, can you say Alec?" Hearing his name spoken evoked his image. Debbie could imagine him here in the room. He would dwarf the kitchen. She pictured him in one of the bright red chairs holding Gino on his lap, bending his fair head close to the boy's dark one. He would entertain them both with some fantastic tale. He would be good at keeping children quiet after the practice he'd had in his father's office. No doubt of it. No argument. Everything about Alec pleased her. "Say Alec!"

"Horse!" Gino shouted gleefully.

Alec's one fault, she thought: his love of horses. She hadn't believed him when he told her that some day she would love them, too. When she learned to understand and not fear them.

"That's pretty smart of you, little imp. To associate Alec with horse." She reached out and pulled him close. "Are you Debbie's clever fellow?"

"Horse, horse, horse!"

"You'd like to ride some more, wouldn't you?" She was amazed that this scrap of a boy could sit a horse so like a veteran rider. "Maybe you'll be a jockey some day. . . . Say Alec!"

"Al, Al, Al. Debbie, Debbie, Debbie. . . ."

"Gino, Gino, Gino!" She laughed.

He reached up and held her face between his hands as she had so often held his. "You are without doubt the most beautiful little piece of man anybody ever saw." She squeezed him until he squealed. "If I'm ever lucky enough to have a child of my own, I hope he'll look exactly like you. And be just as affectionate, and just as mischievous and just as—"

The bell over the shop door tinkled.

Debbie put her cooky on the table, took Gino's hand, and hurried into the shop. Gino attempted to pull away but she held him tightly.

A tall, sandy-haired young man in a silk suit the color of his hair stood just inside the door.

As she stepped through the portieres, he looked up and said, "Good afternoon," in a low, unhurried voice.

"May I help you?" she asked a trifle nervously.

"If my memory didn't happen to be on a more or less permanent vacation, I'd have attended to this sooner," he said with a nice, big-toothed smile. "I'm on my way to the airport. I've got to be best man at a wedding in New York and—you won't believe this—I never even thought about a present until I was dressing to fly East."

Debbie smiled. "Do you know the bride? I mean have you any idea of the sort of thing that would appeal to her?" To Gino she said, "Stand still, darling."

"She's mad about fine antiques. If I can find something to take with me on the plane. . . . I thought an old man ran this shop. You his granddaughter?"

"I'm Debbie Robyne. I take care of his little grandson after school. I'll be glad to show you—"

"I'm Phil Andrews, med student at City College." His light brown eyes traveled over her and Gino, then moved on to cover the contents of the shop.

"Oh, Alec's told me about you. You're going to be in Dr. Belmont's office again this summer, aren't you?"

He nodded, glanced at his wristwatch and said, "I'm in a little bit of a hurry. Let's see what you have about this size." He held his hands a few inches apart.

Though Debbie knew little about selling, she did know what was available. "We have some beautiful old candlesticks."

He negated that by a shake of his neatly brushed head.

"These Christofle silver plates? Good size, too. For a cocktail and an *hors d'oeuvre,* or candy or salted nuts. They can be used for all sorts of things. Gino, angel, don't pull that way."

"What's Christofle silver?" Phil Andrews wanted to know. "Never heard of it."

Debbie smiled. "I haven't the foggiest notion, but when Mr. Fieldson says it, his customers seem impressed."

"What about the things in that glass cabinet, Miss . . . Robyne, isn't it?"

"Oh, *Debbie!*" She laughed. "Nobody but school teachers call me Miss Robyne. I'll unlock the cabinet and show you. Mr. Fieldson's very nicest things are in there." She removed the key from its well-hidden hook and opened the glass doors. She took out several silver pieces and two of the handsomest of the jeweled snuffboxes and set them on a piece of red Chinese brocade on a small desk. "See anything there that appeals to you?" she asked. *How marvelous to be a bride and receive any one of those lovely things!*

Phil Andrews picked up each piece and examined it. His hands were square and strong. His wristwatch as well as his clothes looked expensive. She remembered that Alec had said Phil cared nothing about the pay in Dr. Belmont's office. No doubt he could afford to buy the most costly thing in the shop. *If only he would!*

"Isn't this an exquisite snuffbox?" She indicated the gem of the old man's collection. At that moment she became aware that Gino was no longer beside her. She had released his hand in order to unlock the cabinet! "Gino! Gino, where are you, darling?" she called. She ran to the sitting room, to the kitchen, the bathroom, the backyard. He was nowhere in sight. "Gino, Gino!" she screamed. For a moment she was immobilized by terror. She forgot Phil Andrews. Forgot that the gems of Mr. Fieldson's collection were no longer under lock and key. Forgot everything in the world but Gino and her responsibility. "Gino's gone!"

she shrieked and flew through the shop and out the front door.

She saw him trying to cross Karidale Boulevard directly in the path of an oncoming bus. His scarlet sweater was a bright spot in all the traffic. So little. So uncertain. So immeasurably dear. Her heart gave one sickening thump and seemed to stop beating.

Heedless of her own danger, praying for the boy's safety, Debbie dashed into the street and tried to grab him. Her hand slipped off his shoulder. She plunged forward and threw an arm around his neck and dragged him back just as the great vehicle ground to an abrupt stop.

Automobile tires squealed. Pedestrians shouted too-late warnings. A motorcycle policeman arrived, siren blasting. The policeman on the corner pushed through the rapidly gathering crowd, blowing his whistle and motioning traffic out of the way. People appeared from nowhere, yelling questions, directions, even threats. Bedlam reigned.

And in the middle of all the confusion, Debbie stooped, holding the boy tight against her and struggling to get her breath through the horrible sensation in her chest.

Suddenly, the crowd parted and Phil Andrews appeared crying, "Let me through. I'm a doctor!"

He picked Gino up and spoke to a policeman. "Take the girl to that antique shop. She belongs there." He spoke very clearly and some of those who heard him rushed at once to Fieldson's.

With a supporting arm across Debbie's shoulder, the officer did as he'd been told.

"But Gino," she said, "is he all right? The bus didn't

touch him, did it?" Her voice shook terribly. "I don't think I'll ever get the smell of that bus out of my head." She shivered. "Tell me! Was the little boy hurt?"

Phil Andrews strode ahead of them with Gino in his arms.

"Look, I got a daughter about your age, myself," the officer said. "When I heard that bus stop and got a look . . . made me sick. I tell you, it just plain made me sick. I didn't see *you*, I saw my own girl. She's got dark hair to her shoulders, too. Gave me a mean turn. You're not hurt, are you, kid? I sure hope not. Mighty brave thing you did, you know?"

"I'm not hurt. Not at all. But for some funny reason it's hard to breathe." Debbie tried desperately to keep her voice calm, though she felt as though she had been pulled apart in tiny pieces and put together with a few of the pieces missing.

"Shock." The officer nodded. He practically carried her up the steps and into the shop. "Shock, that's what. And no wonder. No wonder at all." He was very gentle with her.

She noticed a police car at the curb. Phil Andrews and another policeman—very young, very red in the face—were inside with Gino. The officer was in the act of shoving people out of the place, muttering, "Just let there be an accident or a fire and they pop up from underground in droves. You'd think they'd have some respect for privacy. Get on out, the lot of you!"

"I'm not quite a doctor," Phil Andrews was explaining. "I'm a med student about to graduate from City College. I thought those ghouls would let me through if I yelled doctor. May I have a look at both the boy and girl to be sure there's no possible injury?"

A few more people mounted the steps and would have entered the shop had the police not waved them back and barred the door.

"Is there some place . . . ?" Phil Andrews asked.

"Through those portieres," Debbie nodded. "But nothing touched either of us. We're perfectly all right. Examine Gino, if you like. I wish you would. But I'm sure he's not even scratched."

"You ought to get a medal," he said. He carried Gino to the rattan couch and went over him thoroughly. "He's fine. Now, let's have a look at you." He felt her shoulders, her back, arms and legs. "You're okay, too, but I'm sure you'll have a reaction. You've had a bad shock. Don't be surprised if your teeth all ache by night and you feel as though that bus *had* run over you. I'd stick around if I could, Debbie, but I'll have to drive like the old nick to catch my plane as it is. So long."

"Thanks. Thanks a million." Badly shaken, Debbie picked Gino up and sat with him on the couch, rocking him back and forth gently and murmuring words of devotion and gratitude.

17

The Incredible Aftermath

Debbie questioned the red-faced young policeman. "Is that your car parked in front of the shop?"

"Yes, miss, it is." He stood uneasily on one foot then the other. He kept mopping his face with a big blue-bordered handkerchief.

She wondered if this could be his very first assignment.

"Mr. Fieldson ought to be coming back any minute now," she said. "If he sees a police car. . . ." She shook her head. "He'll be simply petrified. I was wondering if it wouldn't be a good idea for you two officers to leave before he returns. In that car," she added with an appealing smile.

The officer who had helped her into the shop spoke up quickly. "You sure are a rare one, kid. Not only brave, but mighty thoughtful, too. You related to the old man? Granddaughter, mebbe?"

She shook her head. She was shockingly tired. It was an effort to talk.

"I don't savvy." He looked puzzled.

Debbie pulled Gino more closely against her. He had begun to wriggle and she wanted to run no risk of his escaping again. "I take care of him," she explained. "Every day after school."

"How come he got away from you?"

"Oh," she said wearily, "I was trying to sell a wedding present to that young man, that doctor, that medical student. . . ."

"You mean the old geezer expects you to be nursemaid and salesgirl, too?"

"Geezer, geezer, geezer," Gino shouted.

"Hush. Darling, please hush." Debbie put her fingers over his smiling lips.

"Well, if that ain't the absolute limit!" the officer said, scowling. "The real, true absolute limit! I'd sure like to tell him so to his face. You're no more'n a kid yourself."

"I wish you'd both go before he comes back. I just did it today, that's all. He's never asked me before but he had to go on an urgent errand . . . business, I guess. Won't you please get out? You don't want him to have heart failure, do you?"

"Okay, Rusty. We'd better beat it like she says. Sure you're not gonna be sick or something?" The officer leaned toward Debbie, his thin, square face tense with concern.

He was probably thinking of his own daughter, hoping that somebody would stay with her in like circumstances.

"I'm fine." She smiled faintly. "Shook up, that's all."

"What will you do if a customer comes?" the young cop asked.

"Shrivel and perish, I guess."

"It's against my judgment to leave you here alone with that jumping bundle of energy," the older officer said. "But we do aim to please. So long, kid. You, too, Gino."

Debbie nodded and thanked him with a tremulous smile.

They departed. The velvet portieres fell together behind them with a soft shushing sound.

With a sudden bound, Gino was off Debbie's lap and making tracks to follow the police, chortling as he ran.

She jumped up and grabbed him and pulled him up on the couch beside her. "You sit still," she said sternly. "Debbie is beat. But good. Don't you move. You hear?"

He regarded her gravely for a moment and touched the frown between her dark brows. "Debbie? Gino good boy."

"You darling! You're not only good but very, very smart. Smart enough, I hope, to stay out of the street. Out of trouble. You must never, never run away, Gino. What if that bus . . . oh, I can't bear to think about it! You stick close to Debbie. Promise?"

His face suddenly crinkled. He batted his eyes. "Bus, bus, bus," he cried, and dissolved in laughter.

Debbie felt that she would never laugh again. She jumped when the bell tinkled. She wondered if she had the strength to go into the shop, holding tight to Gino, and greet a customer with the proper enthusiasm. She was rising from the couch when old Mr. Fieldson barreled through the portieres with such speed and energy that he ripped one of them from the rod in two places.

"I've been robbed! I've been robbed!" he screamed, throwing his hands in the air. "My most valuable snuffbox, the gem of my collection, the one that belonged to Madame Recamier . . . it's gone! And there's another one, and a lot of silver spread all over that desk out there! What's the meaning of this? That cabinet should be locked! Locked, mind you. And here you sit, in the back room, doing nothing, while anybody who wanted to could march in and steal me blind. Get up! Get on your feet and come with me!" He reached toward her.

She wanted to pull away from the touch of his hands. It was impossible to move. She sat paralyzed by shock and apprehension.

The Recamier snuffbox stolen! He would never forgive her. Never in the world. Debbie had seen him fondling that jeweled box as she fondled Gino, with the same devotion. It seemed to have a very special meaning for him. Perhaps he had paid a fabulous price for it. Or perhaps the gems which studded it so brilliantly were more valuable than she had suspected. No matter what the reason. If the snuffbox had been stolen he would hold her responsible. What would she be expected to do? How could she possibly have known what was going on inside the shop when she was in the street saving Gino's life?

"Never have believed it of you," he was saying wildly. "Such criminal carelessness! You'll have to—"

Abruptly, Debbie leaped to her feet, eyes blazing, heart thumping hard and fast. Remembering the crowd outside and those who had rushed into the shop, the theft was not surprising. "You keep quiet and let me tell you something," she said, her words spilling over one another in her haste. "Taking care of this little jumping jack and trying to sell a wedding present at the same time . . . that's more than I, or anybody else, ought to be called on to handle. I haven't told you some of the things I've had to do, taking care of him. He could have broken his neck the other afternoon when we went to get ice cream in the little drugstore on the side street. He simply threw himself at me while we were both sitting on high stools, and if I hadn't been very quick indeed he could have fallen to the floor and maybe been killed. I hurt my back doing it but I didn't care. I wouldn't let anything happen to him if it was humanly possible to prevent it. No, don't you say a word. Not one single word. I've got a few things to tell you!"

The old man pulled a mussed handkerchief from his coat pocket and wiped his face and around the inside of his collar. He was breathing in short, puffy breaths.

"Gino and I were eating cookies in the kitchen when the bell rang. A nice-looking young man in expensive clothes said he wanted to buy a wedding present. Something small that he could take with him on the plane to New York. I showed him the candlesticks, the Christofle plates—oh, all sorts of things. He asked to see those in the glass cabinet. His name is Phil Andrews. I know all about him. He's a medical student and works in Dr. Alexander Belmont's office, summers." Unexpectedly, Debbie had what she would always consider one of her better hunches. "I want to show you something. Come into the shop. No, Gino, it's Grandpa's turn to watch you. Debbie's busy. Come along!"

They all went into the shop.

Debbie picked up everything from the cabinet, restored it, locked the door and hung the key in its hiding place. Then she turned to the old man and said, "Unlock the cabinet." She was too excited to be even faintly amazed by her own temerity.

Mr. Fieldson just stood there with his mouth agape. He held Gino's hand in chubby fingers.

"Well, go on; unlock the cabinet!" Debbie's voice broke.

After he had turned the key in the lock, he dropped the boy's hand. He had to use both hands to open the doors; they had a tendency to stick. Tight. "You expect to find the Recamier box?" he demanded furiously.

"I expect to prove to you that it was impossible to hold onto Gino and open the cabinet at the same time," she snapped.

He shook his head, evidently bewildered by what she was driving at.

"Now you listen, Mr. Fieldson. And listen good. I want you to get the picture. I opened the cabinet and took out those things and displayed them as you found them on that little desk. While I was doing that—it only took a minute— Gino slipped away. The second I missed him, I called. I hunted everywhere, even in the backyard. He was nowhere to be seen."

The old man groaned. Debbie paid no attention.

"Then I tore out the front door and saw him trying to get across the boulevard in all that traffic directly in the path of a bus. A perfectly gigantic bus! I've never been so terrified in my life. I ran out and tried to grab him but my hand slipped. I had to practically throw myself at him with my arm around his neck. I managed to get him out of the way just as the bus stopped. You never saw so much excitement! Police came. . . . Incidentally, I was so afraid you'd be scared to death if you saw a police car in front of the shop that I asked them to get in it and drive away."

Mr. Fieldson sat down hard on a small straight chair almost too small and too fragile to hold him.

"Phil Andrews came, screaming that he was a doctor so the crowd would let him through, and he carried Gino in here. One of the other policemen helped me. People came from—oh, I can't imagine where! Crowds of them. Phil told a policeman to take me in here and some of the people who heard him had the nerve to rush ahead and come inside. I'm not a bit surprised that something is missing. Phil examined Gino and felt my arms and legs and back and said we were both okay. I know it doesn't mean anything to say I'm sorry you were robbed, but I am. My first responsibility is Gino." She was breathless and slightly dizzy. She locked her hands before her in an attempt to steady herself. Never in her life had Debbie talked so fast or in such a mixed-up jumble of words. There was so much she had to make the old man understand.

"I love him. I love him terribly. If anything happened to him, it would just about kill me. I thought I was awfully lucky to make the deal with you about the mirror, and I still do. But I honestly didn't know how strenuous it was going to be. Or," she added on inspiration or hunch or whatever, "that you'd be asking me to do extra, special jobs. Like giving him a bath and dressing him. Keeping shop and Gino, too. It wasn't in our bargain and you shouldn't have expected it. Oh, I was willing enough to help out, in a way. But I hope from now until the end of our agreement you won't ask me for extras again. I honestly don't think it's fair."

The old man sat with his head bowed, chubby hands

hanging together between his fat knees. He said nothing. Made no move.

Debbie began to be afraid he was sick—having a heart attack or something. Such immobility was not like him. Furious and hurt as she was by his censure, she began to realize that shock over his loss was responsible, and she mustn't hold it against him forever. For the moment she had lost sight of her own responsibility concerning the theft.

"Are you all right, Mr. Fieldson?" she asked timidly.

No response.

"Mr. Fieldson, you'd better watch Gino or he'll get away again. It's time for me to leave now. Past time. Darling," she stooped and held the boy, "take Grandpa's hand and hold on tight."

Miraculously, Gino obeyed.

The old man raised his head and gave Debbie the strangest, most penetrating look. It chilled her blood.

At that moment she remembered that in all the excitement Phil Andrews had left without buying a thing. Perhaps that very fact was back of that terrifying expression in old Mr. Fieldson's black eyes. He would have little sympathy with her inability to make a sale. Add that to his dismay over the robbery and Debbie knew that she was in for major trouble.

She hugged Gino, kissed his warm, smooth cheek and then went into the other room for her purse. Ordinarily, she went to the bathroom to freshen up and comb her hair before going home. Today, she didn't even think of it.

Moving jerkily, like a wound-up toy about to run down,

she returned to the shop, said "Good-bye" faintly and started toward the door.

"Debbie!" The old man spoke. His voice sounded odd— sort of choked. Probably with anger. No doubt he was ready to slay her.

She paused but did not turn around.

"I will have something definite to say to you tomorrow. Do not fail to come."

Shaking and sick, she rushed home. She was determined to make light of the afternoon's experience. Her job was in imminent peril. She felt wholly inadequate and abysmally sunk.

18

In the Spotlight

Mother and Dad were having breakfast when Debbie went to the kitchen the following morning.

There was the odor of toast and the aroma of fresh coffee. A band of sunlight turned the honey in a glass jar to golden flame.

"I'm sorry to be late," Debbie began. She noted her parents' expression and said, "What gives? You both look sort of . . . what is it?"

"Sit down, dear, sit down," Mother said. She was bending forward, her face a sparkle of attentiveness.

Debbie glanced at Dad. He was very serious. He motioned her to her chair. She sat down and reached for her glass of apple juice.

Dad took the folded newspaper from his lap and put it at her place. "You'll know how we feel," he said quietly, "when we tell you what we intend to do about it."

Completely bewildered, she picked up the paper. "Who . . . I mean . . . cranberries! I didn't have the slightest idea anybody was taking our pictures!" She didn't know whether to laugh at the absurdity of her position in the picture—

one leg stuck away out and her skirts every which way—or to cry at the memory of Gino's dreadful danger.

"Some enterprising photographer happened to be passing at the height of the excitement," Dad said. "It certainly tells the story." He nodded toward the paper. "You didn't make the rescue sound quite as dangerous as it appears." He touched the photograph with a long finger. "That bus couldn't have been more than three inches away."

He had said they were going to do something about it. Insist that she give up the job? Debbie swallowed the apple juice at a gulp. "The thing I remember about the bus," she said quickly, "is the smell. I can't seem to get the gasoline fumes . . . or whatever it was . . . out of my head. But nothing matters, really, so long as Gino's safe." She hadn't said a word about the robbery. She wouldn't worry Mother and Dad until she knew what Mr. Fieldson was going to demand of her. Surely, everything in the shop was insured. But would the insurance company be responsible when they knew that the door was open and the cabinet unlocked? Debbie doubted it. The doubt sickened her. "I'm not a bit hungry," she said, very low.

"Oh, you must eat your breakfast, dear," Mother objected at once. "You'll have a big day at school, I imagine, what with your picture in the St. Louis paper and all. Did you read the story?"

Debbie shook her head. She couldn't bear to read it, to be reminded of the whole frightening experience. "What are you and Dad going to do? He said I'd know how you feel when—"

"For one thing, I have permission for you to give the

little automobile to Gino," Dad said slowly. "It needs some work and a paint touch-up, but I think the boy will be crazy about it. For another. . . ." He waited a moment while he poured himself another cup of coffee.

Debbie didn't breathe.

"For another, I'm going to refinish the floor in your bedroom."

"And I'll wash and iron your curtains," Mother said quickly.

Debbie struggled against breaking down and bawling. Not crying. Just plain kid-bawling. They were so dear. So very dear not to discuss the danger and their fear for her safety. She jumped up, hugged and kissed them both, and said unsteadily, "Just for that, I'll eat everything in sight! You're both pretty wonderful," she added softly.

Mother asked, as though she couldn't resist the question, "Weren't you frightened to death when you saw the little boy . . . ?"

"Oh!" Debbie exhaled explosively. "I've never in my life been so terrified as when I saw that tiny scarlet sweater bobbing out there in all the traffic. Well, maybe once before, but in an entirely different way. This time my fear was for Gino. The other time it was . . . well, I don't know exactly what. Remember how scared I was the night you took me to that apartment in the city and put me to bed and I woke up . . . ?"

Mother shuddered. "I can still hear your shriek when you looked down into that twelve-story pit of blackness." She covered Debbie's hand with her own.

"We're very proud of you and your devotion to duty,"

Dad said solemnly. "And mighty thankful."

Then the job was secure! Miraculously, Debbie acquired an appetite. She helped herself to a piece of toast and began her breakfast.

She would have given anything in the world not to go to school. Still all "shook up," she was in no mood for an emotional binge. If any of the girls had seen the paper they would ask all manner of questions, want a blow-by-blow account of Gino's running away and her running after him. Debbie didn't feel up to it. But there was no chance of skipping school. *School! How about the afternoon when Mr. Fieldson would issue his ultimatum?* Even though Mother and Dad agreed that she could go on taking care of Gino, Debbie knew deep in her heart that the old man was so angry with her that he was apt to dismiss her pronto. How could she live through the day? How could she bear not to see Gino every afternoon? What about the mirror? Her appetite vanished as quickly as it had arrived. She excused herself and got ready for school.

Cynthia, Ring, and several others were waiting outside the main entrance when Debbie got there. She looked in vain for any of the Muscatels. For Alec. In a way, she was grateful not to see them. Grateful and hurt at the same time.

"Debbie!" Cynthia grabbed her and gave her a violent hug. "You're a real heroine! Maybe you'll get that famous medal, or something. I've never been so thrilled in my life. Why, you absolutely risked your neck, saving that kid. Oh, I'll bet the old man's proud of you! And of himself for having you. He must be *so* grateful!"

"I almost choked on my orange juice," Ring said, "when my uncle asked if I knew a girl at school named Debbie Robyne who had courted grave danger—he said it, I didn't —to save a little boy's life. Golly, Debbie, that's really something! We're all proud as heck to know you, believe me. When I saw that picture. . . . Say! You ought to be tackle on our football team. You and another hundred pounds or so." He gave her shoulder a little shake. His intensely clear brown eyes smiled down into hers.

"It really was horribly brave of you," said a girl in her mathematics class. "Had he been gone very long when you missed him. What were you doing when he ran away? Weren't you scared to pieces?"

"Sa-a-ay," Ring laughed, "why don't you read the story in the paper?"

For the first time, Debbie wondered who had written the account of the near-tragedy, and where he'd gotten the information. From the old man? But no mention of the robbery, praise be.

Between Cynthia and Ring, she entered the building. Some of the pupils shouted congratulations and others asked questions. Ring hushed them all quite effectively by explaining that she was "in no mood for total recall." He and Cynthia escorted her to study hall and left her, promising an award for courage.

Carlotta was alone in the room. Sitting stiff and straight, looking intently at nothing with glazed eyes, like a doll's.

Debbie had dreaded this encounter, the first since the lunchroom scene. Now she had high hopes that Gino's rescue would restore her to the president's graces. With her customary warmth, she said, "Hi, Carlotta!" and waited for her reaction.

It came with shattering promptness. Carlotta whirled to face her and lashed out at her saying, "You've disgraced the Six Muscatels! You know that, of course. A nursemaid! Who ever heard of such a thing? And your picture in the paper with him to boot. With your arms around him hanging on as though he were something very special. Old Fieldson's grandson!" She stood up abruptly and leaned toward Debbie. "You ought to be ashamed of yourself! Aren't you? Aren't you terribly ashamed for everybody in Karidale, and in St. Louis, too, to know about that?" Her golden eyes blazed. Her golden head was thrown back arrogantly. Her exquisite hands twisted cruelly. She seemed to fairly crackle.

Neither girl was aware that the door into the corridor had opened. They had an unsuspected audience of one.

Debbie was afraid she was going to faint. She held onto the edge of her desk with both hands and steadied herself before replying. Carlotta's anger was almost palpable. It seemed to shimmer between them like something alive and threatening. When she was sure that she could speak calmly, Debbie said, "I'm resigning from the Six Muscatels as of this moment." She took a deep breath and continued. "I don't want to be the friend of any girl whose values are so twisted."

"Shut up! You just shut up and listen to me!" Carlotta's face was distorted, all beauty gone. "Why do you think I asked you to join the club in the first place, Debbie Robyne? You're nobody in this town! Your father's just a clerk in a hardware store. You really don't belong with the rest of us. I asked you to join so you'd help me with my French. That's the only reason. The only one in the whole wide world. And it worked, too. Worked beautifully. You've done most of my translating for me, haven't you, you—you *nobody!*"

At that moment, Alec Belmont crossed the room to Debbie. Without so much as a glance in Carlotta's direction, he said, "Debbie Robyne! You're really something!" He took both her hands and held them tight. "Congratulations and all that. I mean it. I've been boasting all over the place that I know you, that we're friends, that you were good enough to let me take you and Gino to my grandfather's farm the other day. The boy's okay, I hope. Debbie, Debbie, you're quite a girl! I'm proud of you. Proud to have you for my friend." He gave her hands a little shake and dropped them.

"Alec . . . thanks." Her eyes begged him to help her. She had been cut to ribbons by Carlotta's confession. Debbie meant nothing to her. Nothing but help with her French. It was unbelievable. It was true.

Carlotta meantime, sputtering mad, was making ugly little noises and slapping books around on her desk.

Not taking her eyes off Alec, thinking even in her humiliation how big and strong, how wonderful he was, Debbie said, "Dad says I may have the little car for Gino. It came damaged and with some paint off. . . ." Alec's look of bewilderment gave her pause. But only for a moment. "I'm crazy about him. You know I am. I want him to have it. When Dad told me about it—they're terribly expensive when perfect—I begged him to see if I could have it for

Gino." She was babbling and she knew it, but perhaps if she concentrated on Gino she would be able to hide her crushed feelings.

Alec, listening with his eyes as well as his ears, said, "Maybe I can repair it for you, Debbie. I could pick it up after school at the hardware store and drive you to the antique shop and your job."

Almost undone by gratitude, she said, "I wonder if I still have a job! Dad says it can be fixed in a couple of hours. The car I mean, not the job."

The room was beginning to fill with curious students who shouted questions, congratulations, and words of praise.

Debbie's face burned. "Alec, take me out of here?"

He took her arm and steered her from the room to a small alcove off the corridor. "Don't be too shook by what Carlotta told you, brown-eyes. Why, the whole school's buzzing with pride in you. That's a fact. You poor kid, it infuriates me for her to talk to you that way. Who does she think she is, anyway? Miss Carlotta Ermine's headed for some real large surprises."

Deeply moved by his attention, his evidently sincere desire to help her in this dark hour, Debbie said suddenly, without the slightest premeditation, "My Aunt Emily's engaged and she and her fiancé—Barrett Fairfax is his name—are coming to dinner at our house Friday night. Will you come, too, Alec?"

Quite obviously surprised, Alec said, "Why, I think I can. Thanks." There was no enthusiasm in his acceptance. He was polite. Period.

Immediately, she regretted the impulsive invitation.

"Look," he said briskly, parking his manner of almost tender concern, "meet me at the side entrance after school."

If he ever asked instead of demanding . . . that would be the day!

Debbie started to ask if he really wanted to go through with his offer. Fearing he might admit reluctance, she nodded, turned away, and returned to study hall.

She got through the day somehow, conscious always of the tearing hurt Carlotta had inflicted.

Alec was waiting when she reached the side door after the final period.

"You look beat," he said. "But good. Car's right across the street. Come on, maybe you'd like a Coke or something at the Rolling Pin." He held her elbow as they descended the steps.

"I couldn't swallow, thanks. It's been quite a day. I'm simply petrified that the old man will fire me." She tripped and Alec caught her arm quickly. On the point of telling about the robbery, Debbie changed her mind.

"Fire you! Don't be ridic, brown-eyes. Of course he won't fire you. Ought to give you a handsome bonus. Hop in!" Alec held the car door.

She got in, settled against the back of the seat and started to laugh. She couldn't stop. It was a bubbly, chuckly sound, half laughter, half tears. She was remembering the first time Alec had given her a ride and how she had looked on that occasion. He would surely think her a damsel in perpetual distress. A gloomy thought. When she had controlled herself, she said, "Remember how I looked the day you took me and the mirror home? You'll think I'm always mussed and beat. Cranberries, but I do appreciate you, Alec!"

He turned to her, smiled, and started the car.

Perhaps she had Carlotta's cruel outburst to thank for the delight of being with him. Had he not overheard their conversation, he would have had no occasion to defend her. She did wish he had been at least a little enthused about coming to dinner. But after all, what sort of a treat would it be for a boy like Alec? He lived on a different scale altogether. Of course, he'd love Mother and Dad, and he'd be crazy about Aunt Em. That ought to make up for simplicity and no maid. She hoped it would. But she wished she hadn't been quite so eager.

In no time at all he parked before the Karidale Hardware Store.

Debbie looked down the boulevard at the colored awnings beginning to appear over some of the shop windows. Sun filtered through leaves trembling in the soft breeze. Their dancing shadows on the street fascinated her. She sat quite still. It didn't occur to her to go in with Alec to get the little car. He had assumed all responsibility.

Almost before she knew it, he had put it in the luggage compartment and was driving her to Fieldson's.

"If you'd like me to wait and see if the old man fires you, Debbie . . ." Alec began. Then he whistled. "That newspaper story seems to have put the antique shop on the map. Take a look at those cars!"

"They can't all be for his shop," Debbie said.

Alec double parked.

"Thanks a mint," she said with her lips and with her eyes.

"I'll snap right into it, fixing up the little bus. See you!"

She got out and Alec drove down the boulevard.

He had been right. The shop was full of customers and more were arriving. The old man wove among them, holding his coffee cup in one hand, and with the other picking up various objects for inspection.

Debbie saw that the cabinet was locked.

At sight of all the people, her heart dropped. Mr. Fieldson was far too busy to pay any attention to her. Business was brisk and so was he. He waved her into the back room without a word and gave his attention to showing a handsome Dresden vase to a woman who looked desperately eager to own it and just as desperately unable to afford it.

If business kept up this way, Debbie would have to wait another twenty-four hours for the old man's ultimatum. Frantic with fear and anxiety, she parted the velvet portieres and stepped into the other room. To Gino.

19

A Golden Evening

On the afternoon of the dinner for Aunt Em and her fiancé, Debbie flew home from Fieldson's on winged feet. Alec was coming! But there was more. She had news. And what news!

It must be saved until after dinner. Nothing should be allowed to intrude upon the excitement of meeting Barrett Fairfax.

He had better be perfect! Aunt Em had had slews of the most attractive bachelors . . . widowers, too . . . crazy about her. If she settled for anything less than the best . . . but of course she wouldn't. A woman of her experience certainly ought to know what she wanted. It would be marvelous to be as sure, as sophisticated and at ease as Aunt Em. Nothing even faintly threatened to rob her of her poise.

Debbie sighed, longing for what Carlotta would call, in her miserable French, *savoir faire:* know how.

Debbie found Mother busy in the kitchen from whence the most tantalizing odors drifted. She looked up, smiled, shoved a lock of dark hair out of her eyes, and said, "Better hurry, dear. You're late. I pressed your yellow dress and laid it on your bed. Your father's in the bathroom but he'll be out shortly. Have a good day?"

"Um h'm." It was all that Debbie dared say. More would almost surely release the secret. "Thanks, Mother."

As she hurried down the hall to her room, she heard Dad whistling under the shower. He was pleased about his sister. He'd been worried for fear she would never marry, and in his mind and heart there was nothing in life to compare with a happy marriage.

It would be fine, of course, if they lived where Debbie could be near them. But the thought of her beloved aunt moving to some distant city was unbearable. She hoped with all her heart that Barrett Fairfax was good-looking. Aunt Em had said "He ain't purty," but she probably meant that he didn't look like one of those slicked-up jobs in magazine ads. He had to be right. . . .

"Your turn, darling!" Dad called, passing her door in a terry cloth robe as white as his hair. "Everything upgrade with my favorite child?"

"Everything okay!" There was an odd intonation in her voice but she didn't suspect it. Nor did she see her dad turn before entering the front bedroom, and give her a quick, slanting look deep with affection and pride.

Debbie looked around the dinner table, satisfied with its appearance. She glanced up at the small gold-framed portrait of Dad's mother on the sea-green wall and smiled. "You'd approve," she whispered. "It's lovely."

Grandmother Robyne's silver candlesticks, polished to gleam like stars, stood on either side of a crystal bowl in which Dad had arranged seven of his yellow roses. Brought to full bloom by the recent rain, they were washed in the hovering glow of candlelight. Mother did not believe in waiting until the guests arrived to light the candles. She wanted to be sure they were going to burn properly. The candles, Debbie thought, giggling—not the guests.

The soft sea-green of the Calyx ware dishes matched the wall. With the Chinese pattern of birds, boughs, and flowers in pastel shades, they were effective on the creamy old linen cloth. Goblets sparkled in the amber light. The unmatched flat silver, all old and much of it worn thin, added its own note of beauty.

As Mother entered the dining room, Debbie turned. "For po' folks, this looks mighty purty, Ma," she drawled. "Mighty purty."

"Did your father go down to the brook again?" Mother asked. "You look sort of purty yourself, dear. I hope he won't bring in a bunch of watercress to be washed at the last minute. He's been known to. That man! You'd think he was part fish, the way he loves to dabble in water."

The doorbell rang.

"You go, will you, dear?"

Debbie looked at her mother, noting how flushed she was and wondering if she was nervous over this affair. *Surely, her insides aren't jigging the way mine are.* The only indication was the color in her cheeks and the unusual brilliance of her long gray eyes. "You look adorable, Mother," Debbie said quickly, and ran to answer the bell.

She hadn't expected Alec. She was all set to welcome Aunt Em and her fiancé. The smiling presence of the tall blond boy in white tossed her for a moment.

"Hi," he said. "Speak up and ask me in. This is the night. Must be, brown-eyes. You're all jazzed up."

"Oh, Alec, I'm sorry," she laughed nervously. "I was expecting Aunt Em. . . ."

"I'll go out and come in later, if you'd rather," he teased.

She pushed at the screen door.

Alec opened it and came into the hall.

Debbie hated herself for being unable to think of anything appropriate to say. He would think her an awkward, infantile goon!

"In that dress," he said, "you look sort of like those yellow roses of your dad's." His blue eyes flicked over her in what she devoutly hoped was approval.

"Dad cut some for the table. They're blooming like fury after the rain the other night. Come on in the living room, Alec." She led the way.

"That's the mirror you went into bondage for," he said, approaching it. "It's a beauty for sure. Looks swell between the windows. I like that scalloped frame. I'll bet your mother was delighted. . . ."

At that moment Debbie's mother entered the room.

"Mother, this is Alec Belmont."

She smiled and held out her hand. "Alec," she said.

"This is awfully nice, Mrs. Robyne." He took her hand and held it for a long moment. "I was looking at the mirror Debbie and I brought home that day. My mother would be nuts about it. She's crazy about antiques."

"It is beautiful, isn't it?" Mother's voice dropped to a near whisper. It always did when she mentioned the mirror.

The doorbell rang.

"I'll get it, dear." Smiling, Mother left the room.

"She's awfully good-looking," Alec said. "But her eyes are gray. Your dad must have brown eyes."

"That's right." Debbie thought Alec unusually observing.

"I suppose he's in the kitchen mixing cocktails."

"He's far more apt to be down at the brook, snagging cress. We don't serve liquor, Alec." Debbie felt her face burn. But he might as well know it first as last.

"Imagine having your own brook and growing your own salad," he said. "Your dad's a real outdoorser. . . ."

"Here comes the bride!" Mother called and ushered Aunt Em and her beau into the living room.

"Hullo, chick." Aunt Em kissed Debbie. "This is your uncle-to-be. . . ."

Debbie took a long look.

"Aunt Em!" she cried joyously. "Remember that TV play about a huge wedding? Remember the bride's father? Oh, he looks like that darling man who took the part! What was his name?" Debbie felt both hands crushed in his.

"Feel flattered, Barrett," Aunt Em laughed. "As Debbie would say, she had a thing about that man."

"To be the *father* of the bride?" he asked. "Flattered?"

Everybody laughed.

"This is Alec Belmont, Aunt Em."

"And this," she said, shaking his hand, "is Mr. Barrett Fairfax."

Debbie studied him as they exchanged greetings. Good enough? Yes, he was. His voice was not as deep and sort of rumbling as Dad's, but it was full and clear with plenty of *umph*.

Dad came in just then with an enormous bunch of cress dripping water all over the place.

"Here's my brother George, Barrett." Aunt Em was obviously proud of them both. "You and your cress!" she laughed.

The men shook hands. Dad kissed his sister's cheek.

"Dad, this is Alec Belmont," Debbie introduced him.

They in turn shook hands.

"Delighted to have you all here," Dad said as though he meant it. "Anyone for cress? Now, Deb'rah, don't you scowl at me! I washed it off thoroughly under the outside faucet. It's clean as water. Good, too." He nibbled a piece.

"Please, sir." Alec stepped up, accepted quite a bunch, and ate it as though thoroughly enjoying it, looking delighted and amused and being very much at ease.

"There's a boy after my own heart," Dad said approvingly.

"Anybody who can grow roses like yours and watercress in his own brook gets my vote every time. This is swell."

"You might pass it, George," Mother said in a resigned way, smiling as though trying to make the best of her husband's off-beat behavior. "Dinner's all ready, I'll call you in a minute." She left the room.

About to follow her, Debbie felt a detaining hand on her arm. She turned and looked up into Barrett Fairfax's smiling green-blue eyes.

He really wasn't handsome, but he had a certain air—an air of knowing what he wanted and how to get it. He was taller than Dad. Heavier, too. Debbie pictured him at the door of a smart restaurant with the headwaiter bowing and offering the finest table available. She thought he was about thirty-eight. Maybe forty. She decided that her confidence in Aunt Em was fully justified. The smile she gave him made him blink.

"Emily told me you were lovely," he said. "I'm sorry my sister Meg could not be here tonight. I hope you girls will be friends, but there won't be much time as she's being married shortly and going to California to live." He nibbled away at his cress, though evidently without joy.

"Is Meg as nice as you are . . . ? Will you excuse me? I want to give Mother an assist. I'm glad it's you she's marrying. Aunt Em, I mean. Not Mother." Laughing, Debbie ran to the kitchen.

"Pour the water, dear, and ask them all to come in," Mother said. "I served the salad. Tossed greens with chicken livers in the French dressing." Her voice was flat—almost angry.

"What's the matter? Don't you like him, Mother?"

"I do wish he wouldn't carry on that way with his blasted watercress! It's embarrassing. . . . He's evidently a man of the world and I think exactly the man to make Emily happy. Of course I like him."

Debbie smiled at Mother's mixed-up sentences. "You mustn't be upset. Nobody else was a bit embarrassed. Everybody loves Dad. I'll pour the water." She picked up the pitcher and went to the dining room.

She heard Alec say, "That slightly bitter taste—swell appetizer," and knew that he had endeared himself to Dad forever. She called them into the dining room.

"The rest of you be seated," Dad said. "My sole contri-bution aside from the cress is carrying in the entrée." So saying, he departed to return at once with a shallow yellow casserole in which six squab chickens snugly nestled, gleam-ing with a wonderful-smelling sauce. "Deb'rah donated her share of cress to the birds, as you see."

Mother had tucked sprigs of cress between them. It added exactly the right touch.

"There's a picture to tempt the gods," Barrett Fairfax said.

Mother came in at that moment carrying another yellow pottery dish. She indicated their seats and they all sat down. "Emily fixed everything. She begged me not to tell, but I'm not about to take credit for such gourmet food. You're go-ing to have to watch your waistline, Barrett, with a cook like Emily in the kitchen. These are string beans, and I can guarantee you've never tasted any to compare with them." She put the dish next to the casserole of birds. "Will you serve them, George?"

"Those little orange things around the beans," Alec said, frankly staring. "I can't figure them out. Everything looks simply elegant. Toledo! I'm glad I was invited! I'd hate to have missed it."

Debbie was relieved that he seemed to be having a good time. At this stage of the evening it was impossible to tell how he had impressed the others. The way he impressed her . . . there were no words to express the floating, un-anchored sensation, the hovering anxiety invading her. It would mean such a lot for the rest to like him, too. He had practically won Dad already, but. . . .

"Those little orange things are glazed carrot balls, Alec," Aunt Em said, leaning toward him with her appealing smile. Her hair was shimmering gold in the candlelight. "Glazed with orange marmalade. And you eat plenty. Carrots are good for your night vision."

Alec laughed. "If my night vision grows any better than it is right this minute, I doubt if I can stand it." He looked from Aunt Em to Debbie and around the table.

His meaning was clear; it pleased everybody.

"Are you in Debbie's class at school, Alec?" Barrett Fairfax asked. "You seem considerably older." He sounded awfully British, broad A's and all.

"Alec's going to graduate in a few days," Debbie said. "I'm just a junior."

"Just a minute, dear," Dad said. "I'll ask grace."

Maybe Alec and Barrett Fairfax would think that terribly old-fashioned or something. But when Dad said Amen the others joined in without hesitation.

"I must tell you an old Yorkshire toast," Barrett Fairfax said. "A short while ago, I spent a night in a hotel in York, where I heard it. 'God bless us all an' mak' us able to ate the stuff what's on this table.' "

Laughter followed.

"There are some splendid hotels in England, of course, but this one was rather uninspiring and the food was formal and quite uninteresting. If ever I have to go back, I shall carry the memory of this Lucullan feast."

"I'll carry it to college, you can bet," Alec said.

"Where are you going?" Dad asked.

"City College. I'm going to study medicine. Dad's an orthopedic surgeon. I'll be in his office this summer with a graduate student, Phil Andrews."

"That sounds splendid," Barrett Fairfax said.

"What am I going to call you?" Debbie asked him.

"What's wrong with Uncle Barrett?" He gave her a winning smile.

"Nothing that I've discovered so far." She laughed.

"Or Uncle B?" he continued.

"Uncle B? Oh, I love that! Aunt Em and Uncle B."

"Sounds like a disarranged alphabet." Mother smiled. She was lovely in a white cotton knit with a string of big green glass beads at her throat and candlelight flickering in her gray eyes.

Debbie remembered that in Katherine Mansfield's biography she had spoken of her mother as "something between a star and a flower," and she decided that that was how Mother appeared to her. Especially tonight with that bright sort of gleam about her.

"This chicken is superb," Uncle B said. "What have I ever done to deserve such a gifted bride, Emily?" He made the name sound like Emilee. The way he looked at her gave Debbie duck bumps. "How about you, my child?" He turned to her. "Have you decided upon a career?"

"I'm going to be a trained nurse," she said emphatically.

"Since she took care of a life-sized doll I brought her from France."

Thank you, Aunt Em. That was so Alec wouldn't think I'd decided after I heard he was going to be a doctor. Oh, thanks, thanks!

"Debbie's crazy about children," Alec said. "She risked her life to save—"

"Oh, Alec, skip it," she begged.

"My child, your Aunt Emily has told me all about it." Uncle B nodded. "I'm proud of you."

"We're all proud of her," Dad said, too loud. "I hope you don't plan to take that sister of mine very far away. Leave a big hole in our lives."

"We've just about decided to settle here. Not right in Karidale—a bit farther out. I want a good bit of land. . . ."

"Oh, wonderful! Marvelous!" Debbie cried, clapping soundlessly. "This is turning out to be a terribly nice party. And, Uncle B, you're just right. Even for darling Aunt Em. That's as big a boost as you could hope for."

Applause followed. As it faded, Mother and Debbie took the dishes to the kitchen.

"Just wait," Mother said over her shoulder, "till you taste the dessert!"

"He's tops, Mother," Debbie whispered, safe in the kitchen with the swing door closed. "Absolute tops."

"Alec Belmont?" Mother asked, not turning around.

"Uncle B!" Debbie cried, blushing furiously. Silently, she added, "Alec, too. Oh, of course. Natch. Absolute tops."

When the strawberry *bombes* had been eaten with oh's and ah's of appreciative rapture, Debbie decided that the time had come to break her news. It had been in the background of her thoughts every single minute, and several times she had been on the point of exploding it.

"I have some news," she said timidly, in the first lull. "It can't compare with Aunt Em's and Uncle B's, but it's sort of exciting. To me, at least." *Sort of exciting! Terribly exciting. Important.* "I have a job for the whole summer."

She was aware of the candlelight fluttering in the soft wind; of the miracle of the yellow roses. Of many eyes upon her. But no one spoke. Not a clink of silver spoon on plate. Nothing. She felt exposed. Ashamed. Well, how could she expect any revelation of hers to compete with news of an approaching wedding? Because it meant so much to her was no reason for the rest to get all hopped up about it. Just the same, she was hurt. Terribly hurt. She had anticipated surprise, delight. Not dull, dead silence. She wanted to ask if nobody cared, but she really didn't trust herself to speak.

Stop behaving like a spoiled kid. This is supposed to be Aunt Em's party. True, you're horning in, but you do deserve a turn. If nobody pays attention . . . make them. Tell all about the job and insist that they listen. Take a deep breath and jump in. You have nothing to lose.

"I'm going to work half-days Saturdays and all day during the week. I'm starting tomorrow. Mr. Fieldson wants me to sell, mornings, in the shop. And take care of Gino, afternoons. He's offered me a wonderful salary. He says he was impressed by my devotion to Gino and the risk I ran to save his life. I haven't told you this before, because I wanted to know what he would do to me, but during all the excitement he was robbed. Robbed of his very most valuable treasure, the Recamier snuffbox. He gave me a hideous bawling out about it but apologized later and said that he and Gino can't get along without me. Even if the insurance company won't pay. They may not, you see, because the door was open into the shop and the cabinet was unlocked." Her breath was gone. After talking missile-fast, she sat gasping.

"I—I'm stunned," Mother said. "Too surprised to find words."

"The old man certainly must be impressed." Dad nodded.

"I'll bet you're the very first girl to land a job for the summer. That's pretty swell, Debbie!" from Alec.

"Congratulations, chick. No into-and-out-of the city. A job within walking distance of home. Oh, I'm so happy for you!" Aunt Em smiled.

"Sounds pretty strenuous," Uncle B said, frowning. "But I'm certain you can handle it, Debbie."

Trouble was, all these remarks were made at the same moment. It took a little while to separate and digest them one at a time. The thing was that everybody was impressed. Congratulations filled and refilled the air. Debbie thought she detected a new respect in Alec's bright blue eyes. Her hurt vanished like dew in sunlight.

"I didn't tell you I'd fixed the little car and painted it fireman red," Alec said. "If it's okay with you, I'll pick you up in the morning and we can deliver it to Gino. Looks pretty good, if I do say so."

Debbie decided then and there that this was the very best party that had ever been given.

When she dreamed later that night, it was not the hideous, terrifying dream of the apartment court twelve stories down. She dreamed about a garden filled with fragrant yellow roses. They were growing in water beside huge silver plates of watercress, each with a lighted candle on it. The beauty and perfume touched her lips and made them smile. Alec was selecting the biggest plate of all. Debbie knew that he would bring it to her.

20

Alec Asks a Question

When Alec arrived the following morning, Debbie and her parents accompanied him to the car to have a look at his handiwork.

Tall and fair, scrubbed and smiling, he appeared more godlike than ever in Debbie's eyes. Her breath came in shallow gasps as she swung along beside him down the crooked brick walk.

With a flourish, he raised the half-open lid of the luggage compartment and revealed the little automobile.

"It's perfect!" Debbie cried joyously. "Fireman red! No sign of damage. Oh, Alec, you—you're wonderful! Thanks a million."

"Good job," Dad said. "The little boy will be crazy about it."

"Why, it's big enough for him to ride in, isn't it?" Mother's approval was in her smile. Then she gave Dad a slight push, urging him toward the house.

As Debbie and Alec drove to the shop, the threatening sky cleared to the deep blue of morning glories. Birds flew bright against it. Wind, bearing the odor of lemon lilies, stirred the leaves of great old trees and threw their dancing shadows on the ground.

"Swell day to go to the Fair," Alec said. Then suddenly, "Let's! You'll go with me."

The air seemed leaping and alert around them. Debbie felt terribly alive. She wondered how Katherine Mansfield would describe the new flavor of their relationship. She turned to Alec and said breathlessly, "I can't! I promised Mr. Fieldson, remember?"

He made no reply. They drove in silence to the shop.

It was closed. They dashed up the steps and rang the bell.

The old man, holding a half-empty cup of coffee, opened the door. "Debbie, child, you're very prompt." Fine drops sprayed from his lips. Black eyes glittered. There was an unmistakable air of excitement about him.

"Mr. Fieldson, you know Alec Belmont. We have something for Gino," Debbie said. Puzzled, she watched him shake Alec's hand with violent cordiality and a mysteriously brilliant smile that seemed to split his face in two.

"And Fieldson got something for Debbie," he announced in pontifical tones. "Before eight o'clock this morning, a young man rang the shop bell and rang and rang until I answered. He paid for the snuffbox! Said you sold it to him, or showed it to him and he decided to buy it. When you called that Gino was missing, he dropped the box in his coat pocket and forgot all about paying for it. . . ."

"Phil Andrews!" His name was a breath of sound from Debbie's lips. "He was flying East that night. Oh, how wonderful! How super! Then you can't blame . . . you weren't robbed after all. Oh, this almost makes up for not going to the Fair with you, Alec. Almost," she added shyly, "but not quite." She was weak with relief.

"You got something for the boy?" Mr. Fieldson asked, still with that face-wide smile. He swallowed the last of his coffee.

She nodded. "What do you have for me? A commission on the sale?" Shocked by her own boldness, Debbie nonetheless managed to smile.

Mr. Fieldson deposited his empty cup on the telephone table. His beady black eyes darted from her to Alec and back. "How's about giving you the day off? You'd like that, eh? Go to the Fair. . . ."

"It's a deal!" Alec shouted. He dashed from the shop and returned immediately with the shining red automobile.

The portieres parted. Gino barreled into the shop. With a wild whoop he launched himself into the car seat as if he'd been a racing driver all of his three years. He tore madly around, shouting and chortling with glee—beeping the horn. His eyes were huge, his cheeks bright pink. "Wizzy, wizzy, wizzy!" he screamed.

"That'll keep him out of your hair awhile," Alec said, laughing.

Debbie explained about the car and tried in vain to capture Gino and kiss him good-bye. He was in a world of his own, unaware of anything or anybody beyond its immediate orbit.

"Come along, Debbie. We'll have the whole day at the Fair. She deserves a break, Mr. Fieldson. Much obliged. Please phone Mrs. Robyne and tell her."

Debbie looked back over her shoulder. Her smile was all

the thanks the old man needed. He held up his hand, fore-finger and thumb joined in a circle of approbation.

A moment later, Alec's car slid from the curb and glided down Karidale Boulevard. Churches, filling stations, drug-stores, and shops flashed by. Then trees, fenced meadows, and gardens. Finally, open country.

Debbie was deliriously happy. "Everything seems to be swimming under pale green water," she said softly.

"Sure!" Alec laughed. "Water's on your brain but I didn't know it was pale green."

Fun. Fun. Fun. This was a choice hour. If only it could be made to last for days, weeks . . . years! Debbie hugged herself and stole a glance at the boy sitting so straight be-side her.

"This is a super car," she said after a moment.

"I'll let you drive it."

"I don't believe I could drive anything so fancy. . . ."

"I'll teach you."

She longed to say, "How marvelous! How absolutely per-fect!" It would sound too juvenile. "Might be fun," she said, as though she had just such offers every day.

"Tell me your birth date, brown-eyes." He was driving with marvelous efficiency.

"July third. I'm almost a firecracker," Debbie laughed.

He shook his head. "Roman candle, with all the lovely lights." He gave his entire attention to driving.

She gave her attention to his remark, savoring it as she would a choice morsel.

Traffic was heavy. Noisy. Cars were full of young people blowing horns and yelling in typical fair-time spirit.

"When's your birthday, Alec? I know you were nineteen. . . ."

"I had a whale of a time last night!" He said it explosively as though the words had hovered long for utterance. "Gay, relaxed, easy time. This may sound odd, Debbie, but I felt more at home at your dinner table than at my own. Mother's a little inclined to pomp and ceremony. You know what I mean."

"I'd be petrified." She laughed, picturing a dining room similar to Carlotta's, and a capped maid serving.

"You'd be exactly what the doctor ordered." Alec spoke with profound conviction.

She sat tense and expectant as though at any moment the car would hit a bump and shatter this incredible dream: She, Debbie Robyne, was on her way to the Fair with Alec Belmont . . . Mercury! She pinched herself.

"Oh!" He snapped his fingers, remembering. "My birthday's the fourteenth of March."

"Well! You're as close to the Ides as I am to the Fourth."

"You're pretty savvy," he said. "I never thought of that. But then," he added, teasing, "I didn't have an erudite aunt living with me till I was twelve years old."

"I know what that means, too . . . erudite." She was not about to correct his pronunciation. She started to hum a popular song. Alec joined in. Before long their voices floated behind them as bright as the colored flags strung on wires above the fairgrounds road. Faint music drifted to the highway. A pale odor of pennyroyal hung on the air. Black Angus cattle huddled in one corner of a white-fenced meadow as though seeking safety with one another from the bedlam around them. Perched on the fence, a meadowlark, its yellow breast bright in the sun, flung its lovely song over the surrounding commotion. Every little corpuscle in Debbie's bloodstream responded to it.

Alec turned right and drove through the grounds to the parking lot beyond.

Music from the carousel, guns popping at the shooting gallery, vendors' cries and the smell—that magical, popcorny, dusty smell—stirred Debbie. She had a sense of ease and warmth.

"It's barely eleven o'clock," Alec said, "but we'd better have lunch ahead of the crowd."

"Fine! I'm starved." Her sigh was not expressive of hunger.

It was hot and dusty. Many of the concessions looked tawdry and tired. Machinery nearby squealed. The big silk tent with signs of the Zodiac painted on it had splits in its sides. The beaded, earringed woman in flowing orange garments seated at the entrance had counted too heavily on makeup to erase the signs of age and dissipation.

Debbie saw none of this. Joy hung a triple veil between her senses and the sights. She actually jumped when Alec touched her arm.

"Her bracelets." He indicated the fortune-teller. "Sort of like yours."

On sudden impulse, Debbie unfastened *Sesame* and dropped it into the woman's broad orange lap.

Smoky eyes lifted. A pathetic smile parted painted lips. "Why, thanks, dearie," a husky voice said. "I can sure use a new one."

Debbie nodded and smiled. They moved away. She turned to Alec and said, "It—it's sort of gaudy, isn't it? I didn't realize it. I thought it was beautiful. Sparkly and brilliant and—and beautiful." Her words were deliberate, thoughtful.

"You'll miss it, Debbie."

"It doesn't mean a thing now. I'm glad for her to have it. For the love of cranberries, the way I starved to get that thing! I adored Carlotta. Just adored her. What an idiot I was! Cynthia Maddern, she was my best friend before . . . well, she *is* my best friend. She told me that Carlotta was making an idiot of me, and I thought Cyn was jealous. All the time it was my French, not me she wanted." Cyn was a doll, and a very happy doll these days, basking in Ring's attention. "She's so beautiful and worldly. Carlotta, I mean. She made me hate being sixteen and—and—well, simple. I longed to be her age, as sophisticated and mature."

"Debbie, Debbie, Debbie," Alec said softly, turning her face toward him. "You don't have to be old or sophisticated to be mature. It's not a matter of age. You proved that to Fieldson when you risked your life to save Gino. And your parents realized it last night when you told about your full-time job. You didn't see the look they exchanged. They might as well have shouted, 'That's our girl! And are we proud!'" Alec took her hand and rubbed her bare wrist. "You proved it to me when you gave away your bracelet. Means you're really through with all the sham and show of girls like Carlotta."

"But you heard me *tell* her I was through," Debbie said, surprised.

"I don't believe everything I hear. But I believe it now and I'm proud of you, too!" He swung her hand.

"Oh, Alec!" It was a heartshaken whisper, too low for him to hear. He had said he was proud of her. *Alec* proud of *Debbie*. It was too much. Too much. After a long, blissful moment, she said, "In a suburb like Karidale, how come Carlotta didn't know what I was doing? I didn't tell her but some of the kids saw me with Gino."

"She did know, Debbie. So did the other Muscatels."

"Not Grace. She'd gone to West Point." But Debbie said it only to herself, taking time in her thinking to wish Grace and her West Pointer well.

"Carlotta made them swear not to say a word to you. She knows you well enough to be sure that if they low-rated your job, you'd do just what you did . . . get out of the club. And she needed you. As long as she could pretend *not* to know— That story in the paper did the trick. She thought she'd lose face if she kept an acknowledged nursemaid in her exclusive club. *She* said it, Debbie. I didn't. Carl told me about it. By the way, she's lost him, too. He began to cool over the way she acted about that long-distance phone call the night of the party. Then the swivet she went into over you . . . that finished her! She's a real. . . . Oh, Debbie, I'm glad you've grown away from her."

"I'm not going to think about it any more," she said determinedly. Nothing should spoil this miracle of a day. It distilled its own elixir which ran like music through her veins.

When they had eaten lunch in a small cafe, Alec said, "I'll buy you spun sugar candy and balloons and striped canes and popcorn balls and get you weighed. We'll have the works. Save the Ferris wheel till last. That's the best."

She would say or do nothing to spoil his fun no matter what the cost to her. If she could meet *that* challenge. . . . Even the thought sickened her. Would she be able to control herself? Everything, but everything depended on it. Did she dare risk it?

Meantime, they ran the gamut of concessions, laughing, chattering, holding hands and loving every golden moment of the golden day.

Finally, the time came to ride the Ferris wheel.

After an argument with herself, followed by a decision which entailed frightful risk, Debbie climbed into the last vacant seat. Alec fastened the protecting rod across her lap and his own. She was more terrified than she had ever been.

The machinery started with a protesting wail. The seats shook. The big wheel began to turn. And as they rose panic, which Debbie had tried hard to deny, pervaded her. She had been afraid on horseback, seated high on gentle Dawn. It was height she feared, not horse. Even being that high in the air had brought back the memory of that apartment court, night-black and terrifying into which she had looked when she was six years old. Not a memory of *sight*, but of *sensation*. A shattering, shuddering fear which she was learning now, to her horror, was utterly beyond her control. She shouldn't have tested her strength. Now, all that she had gained in Alec's favor would be lost. He would consider her weak, childish, infantile. Just when their relationship had acquired a sweet new flavor, this had to happen! She tensed and shut her eyes. Tight. She swallowed the scream rising to her throat. Why, oh, why had she dared?

"Here's the dream world!" he cried. "The very top! You'll love it the way I do. I know you will. Debbie!" His abrupt cry was sharp, ragged. "You're white as—as clouds!" He had turned to her. His breath was against her ear.

If she tried to speak the scream would escape. If she opened her eyes she would faint dead away.

A sudden hideous grinding noise filled the air, followed by an ear-splitting shriek of machinery. There was a world-shaking jolt. Awesome silence followed. No motion. No motion at all. In another moment the whole great wheel would collapse. It couldn't happen soon enough for Debbie. Her panic was worse than death.

"Debbie, I didn't know," Alec said quietly. "I wouldn't have exposed you to this for anything. I thought it was the *horse,* that day you rode Dawn. If I'd dreamed it was acrophobia. . . ." He took her hands and held them close, close within his own. "Just keep your eyes closed, Debbie. You're perfectly safe. I'm holding your hands and I won't let go. It's not an uncommon fear at all. I'll take care of you, Debbie."

His voice was reassuringly calm. His words didn't altogether register. He was trying to help her. That she did understand. He was not laughing at her. There was no scorn, no contempt in his voice.

"They'll get the machinery started before it rains. It's clouding up." He leaned very close to her. "Rain wouldn't bother you. Your face is a clean, sweet little job without a trace of goop to run or smear. That trembling all through your body . . . it'll go away. I know it will. So I'm not worried. Just sorry. Terribly, terribly sorry, brown-eyes."

A megaphoned voice rose from the ground. "Take it easy, folks! Happens once or twice a day. Don't mean a thing. Be on your way shortly. Just a minor repair. Nothing serious. Relax and enjoy the view."

The gay response of the other passengers should have been reassuring. Instead, Debbie felt more of a coward than ever.

"May be a good thing we did break down," Alec said close to her ear. "Keep you up in the air long enough to get the best of that fear. You can do it. I'm counting on you."

Her hands moved within his. The pressure of his fingers increased.

"Alec," she whispered, dry-lipped. "I'll try." *I'll not only try, I'll succeed. I've got to succeed. If I don't. . . .* She would not, could not contemplate the disaster of failure.

The wheel shuddered violently. Machinery whined.

Debbie opened her eyes a tiny bit. Everything around her quivered alarmingly. She closed her eyes. Opened them again. "Alec? I'm looking," she said just above a whisper. "I guess I'm okay. I . . . I'm looking." She said nothing about the awful sickness churning in her stomach or the whirling sensation in her head. She felt with deep certainty that her future could depend upon conquering this fear of high places.

"I'm looking, too," Alec whispered to her eyes. When they reached the ground he said, "We'll have to run for it. It's starting to rain."

She was dizzy and ill but forced herself to keep pace with him. Each time her foot touched the ground she felt better.

They reached the car and got in. As they closed the doors, rain hit the hard top like bullets. Thunder boomed. Lightning flashed.

Their eyes met in the silvery light.

She waited almost without breathing, her heart beating wildly, for a reversal of Alec's approval. He would be anything but proud of her now.

"I'm going to get you a bracelet for your birthday," he said, ducking his blond head toward her. "Perfectly plain. Solid gold. With your initials raised. . . . Tell me your middle name if you have one." His hands were tight-locked between his knees. He looked away from her startled eyes.

"Anne," she whispered, shaken by hope and fear.

"Deborah Anne Robyne. D. A. R. That's the start of a word I've never used. Never. If you're interested you could add four letters and come up with the answer." He turned back to her then and gave her a quick, flashing smile.

She touched her lips with the tip of her tongue but could not speak. Could it possibly be that her fear had not robbed her of his regard? Dared she hope for yet another miracle?

"Well, Debbie, any time you'll say the word, I'll listen. Remember, I said you were your own girl. Well, after the way you fought it out with yourself high in the air, I'd like to say you're mi—" He shook his head, not completing the word. Lightning flashed across the sky and was reflected blue-bright in his eyes. "Don't be so stubborn!" He gave her shoulders a little shake. "You know the word I mean. Say it! Dar. . . ."

"I might say the wrong one." Her voice was light and trembling with joyous teasing.

"Okay, okay, I'll say it! Will you listen?"

Smiling and shivering ecstatically, Debbie nodded.

Alec had asked a question! This was the day!

WHITMAN TEEN NOVELS

"Minnow" Vail

The Charmed Circle

Milestone Summer

When Sara Smiled

Practically Twins

Then Came November

When Debbie Dared

The Wishing Year